THE VALLEY OF TEN THOUSAND SMOKES

by

Mark Webber

DORRANCE
PUBLISHING CO
EST. 1920
PITTSBURGH, PENNSYLVANIA 15238

Dorrance Publishing Co
585 Alpha Drive
Pittsburgh, PA 15238
Visit our website at *www.dorrancebookstore.com*

ISBN: 978-1-6853-7034-3
eISBN: 978-1-6853-7884-4

DEDICATIONS AND FACTS ABOUT FICTIONS

I sincerely dedicate this, my first book, to all my friends and family. I realize that some of my friends and family don't like to read even though they can. So, I'm not going to force anyone to read this. Just knowing that you have it is good enough for me. Though I have written many stories I have never really had anything published so I thought it was about time. With all the gadgets of our time, there are very few things one can give to another person that would be as personal as a product of your own imagination. Though you may be thinking, and I agree, that there are some products of people's imagination that I would not necessarily like to receive.

I actually started this book many years ago. Although I like to write fiction, I thought I would like to keep the facts of the fiction correct. So now the fictions are backed by fact and I have included the facts of the fiction at the end of the book for reference. I think this is the reason that it has taken so long to finish it, all that dang research. That and the world demands that I pay attention to it, which keeps me from actually doing most of the things that I really want to do. I would really like to keep this story going and with a little prodding I hope that I will do just that. So the ending of this book is not necessarily the ending of the story.

The beginning of the book is where I plan to have the end of the story lead and pick up again to bring it to a more modern time. I guess that is why there is a prologue or two.

All the mountains and valleys in this story can be found in or near the valley in Alaska called the Valley of Ten Thousand Smokes.

TABLE OF CONTENTS

CHARACTERS:

The Winged
Colony Boann
Colony Morrigan
Petolemy and Seleucid
Modnar = Guardian
Bob and Dameron
Aguta, Gatherer of the Dead
Ahnah, Woman of Tears
Dambar, Wielder of Tobine's Sword

MEN IN THE MOUNTAIN:

Mount Novarupta: Rulers and Governors, Banden, Barrat, Flagen,
    Barpet, Domage, and Juhle
Mount Mageik: Ambassador Tobine
Mount Martin: Ambassador Unckle
Mount Trident: Ambassador Rockten
Mount Griggs: Ambassador Monglen
Mount Alagogshak: Ambassador Shotgen

THE PROLOGUE STORY

Within the velvety darkness of the night, snow fell silently on the tundra, beginning the season with the first coat of termination dust. Some people have been dreading this day for months. They hate the cold and the long nights of ice and snow. But I love the snow and ice. The long nights filled with dead sound, killed by the freshly fallen snow. The cold brings a new fresh scent to the air and a new beginning for me.

I awoke wondering how many years I have hibernated this time, I thought to myself. I was so sick of everything when I finally decided I had enough and buried myself here. I threw everything away and separated myself from life. I'm truly surprised I survived the separation. Not many Winged have ever survived the separation. I am sick of hibernation and I will not ignore this now that I am finally awakened. By the rebirth of the new season. I can feel the heavy heat leaving my body and my tiredness fading away. My swollen limbs became light and responsive. Beneath me the ground was still frozen and cold, but above me the unfrozen soil was loose. With the newly fallen snow dropping the temperature, it seemed like all around me things were cooling off. Even with the new layer of fresh snow, it was still too warm for me to venture out. For now, I will just sleep until it gets more toward winter. I usually don't sleep in the ground like this. I usually hide myself away deep in the abandoned caves of the Mountain People. Whose acceptance of me was tolerated by the fact that I helped the ones who first began building their great empire. My ventures out left me here at the end of the season and the thoughts of whether or not it was worth it put me fast to sleep.

When I woke, I didn't know how long it had been since the time the temperature had dropped enough so that the once warm loose soil was almost to the point of being frozen. It was time for me to venture out before the loose soil froze, trapping me here for the winter.

Now that my body was no longer swollen by the heat my den was much larger and I could move about. I positioned myself on my back and slowly started picking at the sealing of my den and little by little the soil started to fall on me. I pushed the dirt aside into the far corner of my den. In no time at all I was moving up and out through the loose dirt.

Finally at the surface, I was surrounded by the cold crystals of snow. Starving from the many months of hibernation, I began to enjoy my breakfast of water crystals. The snow was soft and light, with a slight smoky taste to it. These flakes must have passed through some smoke from someone's fire.

Finished with my breakfast it was time to climb out of the snow. This snow must have been fresh. It was soft and easy to climb through. Not even the top layer had been melted by the sun and refrozen by night. Breaking free from the snow was a delight as I sniffed the fresh air of the cool night. My wings folded off my back like an accordion. I stretched them out as far as I could. It was great to be out again. I could smell the faintest scent of someone's fire burning in the distance. Looking down at my arms I realized I was covered in the dirt that I had been sleeping in for so long. I must look like a black oily cockroach, I thought to myself. A cool breeze came out of the north and caught my matted down wings. I had myself a good stretch and let my wings catch the breeze and I began to rise into the night sky.

As I rose into the air, all I could see around me was moonlight bouncing off the snow crystals on the tundra. As I rose ever higher into the night's sky, I looked up and saw a white aurora sweeping the sky. Like a painter with a giant brush painting on the black canvas of night, only to have the white vanish trying catch up to the painter's brush to be painted again, in some archaic pattern.

The brush strokes turned into floating sheets of color as I rose higher and higher into the sky. I chased it, like someone chasing a rainbow. I soon found myself surrounded by it, trillions of little specks of light. There was this sound to the light, like a million bubbles popping a high-pitched pop. A bubble of light would appear and then

2

pop, it was gone, only to be replaced by another. I tried to catch one in my hand, but it seemed to avoid my attempts to grab it. I soon gave up only to have the speck of light move in close to my face. To my amazement it was a small ghostly face with eyes, ears, nose, and mouth. It smiled at me, and as I smiled back it disappeared with a pop. Suddenly I found that I was incased in the lights. As the light shifted its position in the sky, I moved with it.

I suddenly found myself growing tired as if the lights were draining me of my energy. The lights began to change. They went from white to yellow and began to move faster in the sky. Then it was orange, and then green. Entranced by the colorful dance I was doing in the sky I had no idea how tired I was. It was the color of blue when it released me.

I found myself floating slowly toward earth. The faint glow of the sun beginning to make its way over the horizon guided me back toward my origin. I could feel the Earth's gravity pulling me down. The wind that had brought me up was now allowing me to slowly glide toward the ground. It was so nice not to have to flap my wings to slow my decent. I was so weak. I just needed to find a place to rest.

As I came closer to the ground, I noticed a small town and headed in its direction. Most of the town was covered in snow and I could make out a few streetlights here and there. Then I noticed some of the buildings had a great amount of light coming from them while most of them had only a small amount. Not wanting to attract any attention, I picked one of the least lit buildings. I began to flap my wings to stop my decent and circled around the building to see if there was some place to sleep the day away. I was in luck; there was a small hole in the side of the building just below the roof. Silently I glided into the hole. It seemed to be an abandoned bird's nest. It still had feathers in it, the perfect spot to sleep. It was no time at all before I was out like an aurora light.

SAMANTHA

Samantha was a girl who liked to sleep in late. She loved to stay up all night and watch her late-night shows or do some reading before she went to bed. So that night she was up till at least midnight. The next morning for some reason she couldn't sleep in as late as she normally would have.

As she lay in her bed and slowly awoke with the covers pulled over her head. She noticed that the sun's light was not coming through her bed covers. Not wanting to get up to early, she tried to go back to sleep, with little success. *It's not fair,* she thought to herself. *I don't want to get up this early.* It was the weekend and she wanted to sleep in. She knew though that it wasn't too early, more like the sun was coming up late now that winter was on its way. Slowly she peeked through the bottom crack of her covers where they touched the bed. There was something waiting for her outside her covers, and it was close. It was on the bed and sniffing, in short little toughs of breath. As she lifted up the covers ever so slightly, she felt a small furry face with whiskers poke its head under the covers and lick her face.

She reminded herself not to eat tuna melts before going to bed anymore. She retaliated by quickly snatching up Furball and holding him close to her under the covers. The cat let out a short squeal of a plea to be set free. Samantha loosened her tight hold of Furball and the cat shot off onto the floor and out her bedroom door. Still disappointed that she had woken up too early, she rolled over. Now facing the direction of her bedroom window, she could make out the faintest light of the sun just beginning to rise but still behind the great mountains that surrounded her little town. She slowly crawled out of from beneath her covers just a bit, to look outside of her window. Almost all of the trees had lost their leaves. There were a few dried brown leaves on the ground. Some of the leaves were the size of maple leaves but only dried up and kind of curled inward. There was one leaf that kind of looked like a frog with its ends curled underneath it like legs. It suddenly came to life hopping around on the ground as the wind picked it up and moved it about in a big circle. It came to rest almost in the very same spot where it began its short journey.

The presence of dry leaves on the ground meant that winter was on its way. Her eyes then turned upward toward the mountains as the smell of bacon drifted slowly into her room. The snow line in the mountains was dropping lower and lower every day now. She noticed that the sky behind the mountains was slowly turning pink as some clouds came between the rising sun and the mountains. *Hope it snows soon,* she thought to herself. She then heard her mother calling for her. "Samantha?" she called.

"Yes mom!" she replied.

"Breakfast is ready!" Samantha hesitated for a moment, what would be better, staying in bed or having breakfast? She thought. The smell of eggs now joining forces with the smell of bacon concurred over the warmth of her comfortable bed. She sunk under her covers and turned around and poked her head out the other side of the covers to look for her slippers.

"Furball!" she yelled. "What have you done with my slippers?"

A high-pitched but guilty sounding "Mmmeow!" came from just the other side of her door. Samantha turned her head toward the door and saw her slippers there in front of the door, blocking it from opening any further. Throwing back her covers she sat up and focused her eyes on the now slightly shredded fabric of her slippers.

"My new slippers!" she growled. "You're going to get it cat," she declared as the sound of tiny foot falls galloped down the hallway toward the kitchen. Samantha's feet found the floor and made their way into the slippers. She opened her door and walked down the hallway and into the kitchen. "Good morning mom," she said.

"Good morning," her mother replied, opening one of the many cupboard doors that surrounded the kitchen Samantha pulled out a glass and headed toward the fridge. She quickly pulled the fridge door open and looked for the bottle of orange juice.

"Mom! Is there any orange juice left?" she asked as her eyes passed over the days old leftover turkey, mashed potatoes, candied yams, and mincemeat pie.

"Yes, behind the eggnog," came the reply.

Moving the eggnog aside, almost causing an avalanche of leftovers to come down on the floor, Samantha quickly grabbed the orange juice and headed to the kitchen table. Shutting the fridge door with her foot, her mind began to think of what she was going to do today. She pulled out a chair and sat down. She then poured herself a glass of orange juice and set it down on the table. Her mother then came up from behind her and set a plate of over easy eggs, bacon, and toast with salmonberry jelly on it. Samantha picked up a fork that had been previously placed on a napkin upon the table. Her eyes studied the plate of food.

Pondering where to start, her eyes lost focus on the plate and began to focus on some strange figure across the table. A small furry head with bulging eyes and radar like ears had centered all their attention on what was on her plate. Furball had jumped up onto the chair across from Samantha and sat there watching and hoping for a handout. "No way cat!" she murmured.

Just then the kitchen door that led down to the basement opened and her father emerged from the darkness carrying a box. "Good morning!" he said as he placed the box on the table next to Samantha. Samantha peered into the box as she started in on her breakfast. It was full of wires and lights of all different kinds of colors. "Anyone going to help with the lights this year?" her father asked.

"I can't," said Samantha's mother. "I'm baking pies today."

"How about you kiddo?" he said as he rubbed the top of Samantha's head with his hand.

Hmm! she thought to herself. The politics of this time of year was a must to be played in order to get what you want at that special time. Samantha's face lit up as she said, "I would love to help you dad!"

"Okay then," replied her father, "get dressed when you finish your breakfast and we will hang these lights up outside before it begins to snow."

By the time Samantha had gotten dressed and had made it outside, her father had already gotten the ladder up and was stringing the lights. She ran over to him and picked up the box that held the lights and began to feed her father the string of lights as he needed them from the box. Every now and then she would encounter a small snag and would have to untangle it before her father could hang it up. Somehow this task took forever. Stringing a foot or two, then moving the ladder and stringing another foot or two. On and on it went until the entire trim of the house was decorated in multicolored lights. Then it was the windows. However, the ladder only needed to be positioned once to encompass the entire window with lights. The house was pretty much in the shape of a box, and it had several windows on each side. There was a window for Samantha's room on one side, and the next window was the kitchen window, two windows for the family room, two windows for the dining room, and two for the garage. By the time they were almost finished the smell of cherry pies had begun to fill the air. The sun was on its way down and the time had come to plug the lights in and marvel at their work. Her father plugged the final plug and went over to flick the switch. Clouds had completely covered the sky and the sun was on its way down. The perfect time to turn on the lights. Her father flipped the switch and Samantha anticipation led to disappointment when only half the lights came on. Her father joined her and looked at the lights. "Ugh!" he said. "Looks like I'm off to the store for replacement lights."

Samantha walked to the front door and her father toward the garage and to the car to make the trip to the store. As Samantha opened the door, the smell of cherry pie was very strong. "Mom!" she said. "Could I have some pie please?"

"Not till you have some dinner," was the reply.

"What's for dinner?" replied Samantha.

"Leftovers," stated her mother.

"Again?" replied Samantha.

"Yes honey, we have to get rid of this food first before we can fit anymore in the refrigerator. Don't worry I will fix you a plate. Just give me a few minutes." Samantha slowly made her way down the hall toward her room, closely followed by Furball. She hung her jacket up in her closet and threw her sweater on the bed. Furball jumped on the bed and curled up on the sweater. Samantha rubbed Furball on the head, went down the hall to the family room and flopped in front of the TV. Her mother made her a plate of turkey, mashed potatoes, gravy, and a dinner roll. "Dinner!" her mother sang to Samantha. Walking over to the table Samantha's eyes glazed over the plate and then to the opposite side of the table to see if Furball was sitting in the seat across from hers. She knew that the cat wouldn't be there though, because Furball hated leftovers just as much as Samantha did.

As Samantha finished her dinner, she listened to her father's car pull into the garage. Samantha got up from the table, thanked her mother for dinner and went into her room to put on her sweater and jacket. Stepping outside she noticed that it had been snowing. There was a small amount of accumulated snow on the ground. Her father came out from the garage and handed her an opened box of new lights. "Hand me the lights when I need them," her father said as he climbed the ladder. Samantha pulled out one of the lights in anticipation of her father needing one. She liked these lights. They were larger than the ones that the neighbors used. They were almost the size and shape of a small egg and were really colorful. Soon all the lights were in place and Samantha and her father were inside. Samantha had settled down in her room with a good book and her parents were eating dinner together. Every now and then Samantha would look toward her window to stare at the multicolor lights burning outside her window. Before she knew it her parents were calling it a night. It was only a few more chapters later until she was fast asleep with Furball at the foot of her bed.

AWAKENING

I don't know how long I was asleep. I was resting peacefully when I felt a surge of energy go through my body and all my muscles tensed up in a strange way. It was so annoying, soon it went away and I tried to go back to sleep. As soon as I started to go back to sleep it happened again. I went through this little cycle a few times until I decided that I had enough of it and should get up from my rest. I slowly opened my eyes only to see this bright light shining through the hole that was the doorway to my newly found nest. I thought it was the skylights again and panicked. I shot out of my digs hoping to see it, only to do a full body plant right into a light. My wings followed behind me wrapping around the light like a blanket. With a knee jerk reaction my wings flew back, my body followed and right back into the nest I went. What was this, I thought? I slowly poked my head out of the hole and looked at the light. I then looked to the right and there was another light, only this one was blue. I turned my head to the left and there was another light only this one was green. These lights seemed to be connected by some kind of vine. I followed the vine with my eyes to another light and then another light. There were many lights on the vine. More than I could count. This was not good; I didn't like lights shining in my nest. I had to do something about this, I thought to myself. I flew out of my nest avoiding the light and felt the cool night air all around me and noticed that there was a snowflake falling every now and then. I started toward the white light just outside the nest. I hovered close to it and poked at it with one of my hands. It seemed hard and had a little heat coming from it. I then pushed on it and it moved just a bit. When I stopped pushing it, it went back to its original position. So, I wrapped my whole body around it and tried to fly down to pull it off of the vine.

I went down just a little ways and the darn thing slipped out of my grasp and it went up as I went down. Straight into the snow. I laid there for a moment, thinking. I shot straight out of the snow toward the light. I grabbed onto it with all my might and flapped my wings to the left, then to the right, and back to the left again as hard as I could. Suddenly it began to move, slowly at first and then it went around once, twice, three times and finally the fourth time it went around it went dark and broke free of the vine. It startled me at first having the light go out. But when it broke free I knew I had beaten it. I flew high into the sky with it, over the house that had all the lights around it. There was no way I was giving this annoying light back to the house, so I flew over the road that led to the house and threw the light down to the road. When it hit the road it made a loud popping sound followed by an ever so faint tinkling sound. I couldn't believe it. I loved that sound. I had to do it again. I flew immediately to the blue light and began tugging to the left and to the right and to the left again till it started to turn and eventually came loose. I flew up even higher than the last time and when I released it, I followed it almost all the way down hovering just above it to hear the popping tinkling sound even better than before. What a wondrous thing this was.

"AGAIN!" my mind ordered my body. My soul had lost control of my mind and body. Without hesitation my wings took control and I found myself at the green light. I don't even remember having to fight with the light to get it free. Up I flew even higher into the night sky. I let loose the glass bulb and raced down to the ground passing the bulb on its way down and waited for it on the street below. *POP* went the light and again and the wondrous tinkling sound sent a tingling sensation from the bottom of my spine to all the tips of my body. Before I knew it all the lights on the one side of the colony were gone. I was on my way for another when I had to stop. The worst thing about it was that I didn't stop because I had enough of this wonderful thing. It was because I had the terrible feeling that I was being watched.

FURBALL

Everyone in Samantha's house was fast asleep. It was well into the night when it was time for Furball to make her rounds of the house to make sure everything was okay. She sniffed Samantha and then jumped off the bed. She made her way down the hall and to her food and water dish. Sticking her paw into her food dish, she fished out a piece of dry food and ate it with a low crunching sound. She sniffed at her water bowl and then jumped onto the counter. She made her way to the fish tank that sat on top of the counter. She sat up and put her front paws on top of the fishbowl and began to drink the water from it. Next stop was mom and dad's room. Furball jumped off the counter and headed down the hall to the doorway across from Samantha's bedroom. She quietly entered the room and jumped onto the foot of mom and dad's bed. Furball walked down one side of the bed and up the other sniffing each person as she walked around to the foot of the bed. She looked to the floor and thought about jumping when an ever so slight rustling sound caught her attention. She looked back to mom and dad and then to the floor. Jumping to the floor she was thinking that she had to find out where that sound was coming from. She made her way to the hallway and sat between the two doorways. She sat there facing down the black void of the dark hallway. Ears rotating, one front, one back, and then alternating them until she picked up the sound again. She made her way into Samantha's room and jumped onto the bed. She heard it again and it was coming from just above the window and it was outside. Slowly she walked around Samantha and to the other side of the bed where the window was. She sat up a bit and pushed her nose between the curtains and the wall till it opened up enough to where she could jump onto the windowsill. Again, the rustling sound came from up above. Furball crouched down low and looked up toward the lights where the sound was coming from. A look of astonishment came over the cat's face. Her jaw almost fell off of Furball's face. She froze stiff like a statue. The only thing moving was her eyes. Trying to figure out what she was looking at. It looked human only small with wings like a butterfly. Each wing was the size of the main body. It seemed to be a male of the species and had dark skin with gray edges. Its wings were almost white like snow with dark roots sprouting through them. She didn't know why but the thing seemed to be quite attracted to one of the lights that were surrounding the house. Suddenly the thing flew off with the light. Up into the sky, Furball watched it go. Then the light came down. A faint popping sound could be heard through the window as the bulb came down out of the sky. Then the thing was upon another light. And the same thing happened again. Furball gave a low growl after the second popping sound.

Soon Furball's head was moving back and forth, back and forth as the lights began to disappear from the house and explode on the street. Suddenly it stopped in mid-flight on its way for another light bulb. It looked down toward Furball. The cat crouched even lower, almost becoming one with the windowsill. Furball gave a very concerned meow and leaped off the windowsill as the thing came flying down to get a closer look at Furball. Samantha was lying on her back when Furball came out of the windowsill and onto the unsuspecting Samantha, landing right on the middle of her stomach. "Fuuuurrrrballl," Samantha yelled with what remaining air she had left in her. "Damn cat," she murmured as she rolled over and tried to get back to sleep.

WINGED

I looked back to where my new home was, and then down a bit. There I saw this big smokey brown fluff of fur almost like a tiny little bear cub only with pointed ears and two almost humanlike eyes. I swooped in to get a better look, but as soon as I did. It disappeared.

It had stopped snowing and I was getting weak. I needed some kind of replenishment. I flew just above the house and looked around. I noticed that there was a frozen waterfall higher up in the mountain just behind the house. I decided this would be a good source of energy for the rest of the night. So, I made my way on up. Higher and higher I went. At first it seemed like a small waterfall but it got larger as I got closer. The moon was out and I could see its rippling reflection within the waterfall. Its surface was such a random form of coarse and jagged glass finish. When I finally reached it, it was like standing in front of myself with the moon behind me. I had to admire myself and run my hands through my snowy white hair. I gave myself a toothless grin, as I closed in on the frozen water. I plastered myself against the waterfall taking in all of its icy warmth. I seemed to almost exchange powers with the frozen water. It charged me with energy and in exchange I changed its molecular structure. It went from a clear ice to a slightly green tinted ice. I moved along the ice in a horizontal direction. As I moved along I noticed that my effect was different as I moved about. Some of the ice turned an almost milky white and other parts turned almost blue or brown. Once it had turned its colors though, I could no longer absorb any more of its nutrients. I would have to find every waterfall in the area if I expected to make it through the winter. After refueling I flew to the top of the water fall and sat on a rock that was in the middle and looked over the small town down below. What wonderful lights. I thought to myself as I looked down at the city. I wonder why I am here. What is my reason for being this time? Am I good or am I bad?

I guess in some eyes I am bad, and others I am good. I wondered what I was in the eyes of that ball of fur that I saw tonight. The moon was now falling behind the mountains and I thought to myself that this would be a good night to figure things out. As the moonlight faded from the night's sky waves of green lights came from behind the mountains, crashing onto the shores of a midnight sky. I wondered if there were any more like me or if I was the only one. When I saw the lights in the night change from green to blue I knew that I was not alone. Sadly, though that did not resolve my reasoning on why I was here or why any of us were here. For some reason I did not care if there were others like me. I kind of liked having my own grounds. I felt the winds pick up and I felt the need to go down to the house where I had been before. I spread my wings and caught the wind. As I rose into the air I suddenly felt a sense of purpose and knew that this would be a good season. As I approached the house I could almost see the heat leaving the edges of the snow coated house. The snow seemed to be black and the edges of the house turned a light red. My eyes were changing as I was getting stronger. I knew that many things would change. I no longer desired to live in the hole that was on the side of the building. I needed the cold and decided I would build a small nest of snow on the top of the house. The snow on the house was hard and windblown. Using the tips of my wings I was able to cut squares out of the hard packed snow. First I built four walls, a cube of snow for each side. Then I placed a fifth block on top for the roof and cut a small hole in one of the walls for a doorway. After finishing my home, I stepped back and studied my work. I thought to myself that it would do. I looked into the night sky. There were clouds on the horizon and the sun was on the way up. Even though it would be hours before the people in this house would be able to see it. I knew it was time to take advantage of my new home. I flew back up to the waterfall and broke off a small chunk of the frozen water and flew back to my home. I crawled inside and placed the chunk of ice in the center of my humble home and curled up next to it for a nice long nap.

ANOTHER PROLOGUE

Long before the sun rose the sky above was filled with a thick blanket of clouds. The air was still and not a hint of a breeze could be found. Snow was falling softly when Samantha began to awake that morning. She was surprised to find that Furball was not in her usual spot. "Furball?" Samantha sang in a soft voice, "Furrrrrbaaaalll," she sang again. A soft meow came from under her bed. Samantha sat up in her bed and then bent over the side to look under her bed. Furball's eyes perked open wide when she saw Samantha's hair brushing the floor. "What are you doing under there?" said Samantha. Furball sat up and gave a soft *meow?* as if to ask a question. "Let's go get some breakfast," said Samantha. With that said, Samantha sat back up on her bed and then jumped to her bedroom floor and quickly got dressed. She took a quick look at her bed and then headed down the hall to the kitchen. It wasn't till after Samantha had left the room that Furball poked her head out from under the bed, and then started down the hallway, hugging the wall as close as possible. By the time Furball had entered the kitchen Samantha was already halfway through a bowl of cereal. Furball followed the wall around until it came next to Samantha's chair. Only then did Furball peel herself away from the wall and sit under Samantha's chair. Samantha's eyes wandered from her bowl as she finished her cereal and looked out the window that was directly across from the breakfast table. *Snow*, she thought to herself as she witnessed the lights from the house lighting up the soft white snowflakes falling in front of the dark sky. Her mind drifted from snowmen to sledding, snowboarding, and then finally to snow shoveling. She wondered how much snow had fallen. If there was a great amount of snow then her father would remove it with the snow blower, but if it was just a little then she might be able to earn some money by shoveling it herself.

Just then she heard a creaking sound just above her head. Something or someone was on the roof. Furball peered out from beneath the chair and looked up to the ceiling. Samantha heard a muffled "Hey! Look what I found," come from up above, which was followed by a big thud and some ceiling dust. Looking back to the window across the room she saw a roof full of snow fall to the ground followed by her father. She quickly ran outside to see if her dad was okay. She ran outside the front door and rounded the corner of the house to see her father buried headfirst in the snow with his legs sticking straight up out of the pile of snow. Stifled by the snow, Samantha could hear the long string of choice words her father was using to express his gratitude for still being alive after that. Quickly she began digging her father out and in no time at all her father was sitting upright in the snow clutching tightly in his hand what he had found on the roof. "I knew it," he said. "I've been looking for this since last summer." He was looking at the hammer in his hand like it was its fault for being up on the roof. He had made a few repairs to the roof that summer in preparation for the following winter and left it on the roof. "Thank you honey for the help out of that snow pile," he said.

"No problem," she replied. "Dad, is it okay if I take the snowmobile out to the glacier and back?"

"Hmmm," looking up into the snow-filled sky he thought of the weather conditions for the day. "It's snowing pretty well now," he stated, "but it is supposed to clear later. So, I guess it's okay."

"Woo-hoo!" Samantha squealed and darted for the garage.

"Just make sure you have enough fuel and do all the safety checks before you take off."

"Okay Dad!" she shouted as she rounded the corner to the garage. It only took one twist of the handle located in the center of the garage door and it was shooting up and into the overhead of the garage. To the right of the car was the snowmobile covered with a tarp. In no time at all, Samantha had the cover off and the engine running. She then went to the back of the garage and underneath her dad's workbench was the bag full of snow bibs, coats, gloves, hats, and gloves. She took her time and made sure that she had everything on right and to give the snow machine time to warm up. After suiting up she went inside and to the kitchen and gathered together in a ziplock bag a half dozen cookies and some cheese for the road and dashed back into the garage. Her father was waiting for her in the garage next to the snow machine.

"Be back in a couple of hours," he said. "And if you're not I'm going to have to come looking for you and I'm not going to be happy."

"Yes, Father," she replied. She revved up the engine and slowly moved into the driveway and out into the street. She felt the rush of adrenaline as sound of the snowmobile coupled with increase of speed, as she reached forty-five miles per hour in no time at all. She came to the end of her street that connected to another road. She came to a stop, stuck out her arm, and made a left turn. Her mind went into a blissful state as she gunned the sled, letting the houses on either side of her become a blur of colors. Soon she was at the end of the road and the beginning of a trail that would take her to the shrinking glacier. There had been other sleds out here already. She could see their tracks. The snow was packed and firm. There should be no problems and at some points she would be able to open the machine up. It was only a two- or three-foot snow ramp up from the street to the snow trail. She slowed down and went up the embankment. Now on the trail she squeezed the throttle and went as fast as the trail would let her go. The sound of the sled seemed to disappear as she went down the path. She stayed mainly on the trail but sometimes she would look off to the side and see the fresh snow and would swerve off the trail and parallel it for a while, enjoying the feeling of floating around on the snow, before returning to the hard packed trail. It was almost five miles to the glacier but it seemed to only take minutes to get there.

The trail she was on was a glacier fed river during the summer months. During the winter months it freezes on top. The snow machines then use it as an access trail to the glacier. Samantha loved the thought that underneath her was a flowing river. The snow had stopped and the clouds were starting to fade, just like her father had said. The glacier was now in sight. She was on a straight away now and there was no one on the trail. She squeezed the throttle and the front end lifted off the snow and she took off. She was at the face of the glacier in seconds. Keeping a safe distance, she marveled at the sight of the glacier. The sun was out now and it was beginning to set behind the glacier. The hundreds-of-years-old ice was a deep blue. The crevasses that let the sunlight in lit up some of the blue ice. The beams of light seemed to dance like crystal marionettes in a sea of blue. Sometimes it would get into the eighties in the summer and to the people around here that's sweltering. So, people would come to stand near the glacier to cool off.

She had been out here many times in the summer and she had never seen the glacier quite like this. Samantha was thinking that the summer heat must have melted the glacier back to some kind of special ancient ice, hundreds of years old. Its blueness seemed almost to be magical. Samantha got off her sled and sank up to her knees in the snow. She wondered how far down the ice and water was. Slowly she walked, or more like trudged, through the snow. Without thinking she stopped and pulled out her bag of cookies and cheese. She was content where she was for the moment and gazed at the ice while she had her lunch. When she was done, she put the bag into her pocket and resumed her slow pace to the glacier. Once she reached it, she studied the glacier ice. She noticed that some of the ice had stones imbedded within it. One of the stones caught her eye and she noticed how different it was from all the other stones. She pulled out a Swiss Army knife that her grandfather had given her. She quickly began to chip away at the frozen blueness until she had a fair-sized chunk of history surrounded by aged ice. She placed it in her bag that she had stuffed in her pocket and proceeded back to her snowmobile.

Once she was back on the trail and returning home the sound of the snow machine became distant to her. Her eyes were focused on the trail as she navigated it with precision. She felt as if there was a window that had been opened up in her mind. The snow machine seemed to begin to float as if she was riding on a cloud. Looking down at the instrument panel she noticed that her speed was 110 mph. She calmly let off the throttle to slow down. Though she was extremely frightened that she was going faster than she had ever gone in her life, she felt very calm. She never wanted to do that again but in the same instant she knew that it would not be long till she would be giving it another go. It was as if she was having two sets of thoughts going on at the same time. The rest of the way home she had to remain focused to keep at a steady safe speed. When she arrived home, she put the sled away and went inside. As she entered her home, she noticed that it was very hot. It was so hot that she began to sweat. "Mom?" she called out. "Why is it so hot in here?"

A distant reply of, "It's not hot in here, take off your jacket," came from one of the rooms in the house. She took off her jacket and put it under her arm. It seemed to make it even hotter. As she went down the hallway to her room she stopped to look at the wall thermometer. It read sixty-five degrees. She couldn't believe it. Feeling the sweat dripping down the center of her back she turned around and stormed out the front door. Once outside she sat on her front porch and enjoyed the cool winter air. Soon her mind began to drift and that feeling of a window opening up in her mind came back. She began to look up to the sky. She looked up higher and higher, until she was looking straight up. When suddenly she noticed the Christmas lights that decorated the edges of the roof. She wondered why she had never really noticed them before. All the different colors and their shape. Not round, not oval, more like *rouval*, that is what they were shaped like, *rouval*. She had to touch one. She stood up and put on her jacket. She reached as far up as she could on her tiptoes. She could hardly reach one, but she did and unscrewed it from the socket. She studied it carefully and then without even thinking she threw it into the street. *POP tinkle tinkle* went the light bulb. What a wonderful sound she thought. She had to do it again. Once she had another one she went into the middle of the street and threw it straight up so that when it landed it was right at her feet. *POP! Tinkle tinkle* went the bulb again. Oooooh! She thought. Just one more. Soon half the front of the house's string of lights were gone and she was standing in the middle of the street with about five in her hands. She was going to throw them all at once, in one glorious moment, when suddenly she felt as if she were being watched. Looking down she noticed Bradley, the neighbor's five-year-old son grinning ear to ear. He was just waiting for her to throw the hand full of lights. She put the lights in her jacket pocket and took off her jacket. She began to feel very cold. Her teeth were chattering.

"What on earth?" came from her father as he stood on the front porch. He marched over to her and picked up her jacket. He looked straight at Samantha and said, "Now I know what happened to the string of lights on the side of the house. Now you go straight to your room and stay there until I can figure out what I'm going to do about this." She walked slowly to the house, very cold and not quite sure what had just happened. Her father watched her go into the house and then looked down at little Bradley still grinning from ear to ear. "Don't even think about it," came from Samantha's father, wiping the grin right off of little Bradley.

IN THE BEGINNING

The room was dimly lit by a small crystal in the center of the room. An old tree stump standing by its roots in the center of the room was its mount. The stump was whittled into a wooden spring coiling its way up. Starting on the outside of the stump it curled inward, up, and to the center, a perfect perch for such an item. The room was carved out of rock and the floor was dusty from lack of use. The only way in was from a hole up in the top of the rooms corner. The room was at the bottom of a tunnel one hundred yards up, with only two other rooms on each side of the long tunnel, which went upward at a forty-five-degree angle. Both the tunnel and the rooms were carved out of solid rock. The walls were smooth and polished to a shimmering perfection. The mouth of the tunnel was guarded by a moving glacier. Shimmering blue lights from the sunlight passing through the glacier ice danced to loud sharp cracking sounds. When a large crack was formed in the glacier a sound much like that of a shotgun would ring out and echo out for miles. The wind that passed through the crevasses seemed to be calling for the keepers of this Hollow to come home.

It was the beginning of winter and the time the sun spent casting its rays on the massive glacier guarding the Hollow were short. As the temperature dropped they began to rise. Rise up out of the dirt like some kind of living dead coming out of its grave or like a vampire awakening from a long dirt nap. They are few in numbers, only maybe a few hundred or more, but they have always been here. None are born and only a few die. Like a mistake that someone had made and did not want to perpetuate. They are as they have always been. Soon the Hollow will be full of them. After they have all awakened and assembled, they will decide on what they will do while the season lasts.

The Hollow was ruled by two colonies, the colony of Boann and the colony of Morrigan. In the beginning of the union of the two colonies Seleucid and Petolemy, being the leaders of each colony, were the two appointed to guard the crystal, and to rule each colony. Being the largest and the wisest of the two colonies and the only two to ever survive the grip of the crystal, they would be the unstoppable forces guarding the crystal and enforcing the Law. The Law of the Crystal is that there is one soul for the power and one crystal for its soul.

Petolemy of the colony of Boann was the first to rise from the tundra. His pale bluish-gray skin creased as the dark muscle tones of his body seemed to reenergize in the cold night air. His eyes turned into the direction of the wind, reflecting the black of the night like a mirror. His white hair seemed gray in the night. His thin metallic armor designed to enhance the cold made an eerie sound as it whipped in the wind. His wings stiffened. Catching the wind in his wings he began heading straight into the night sky and toward the glacial hollow. Seleucid of the colony of Morrigan was next, pausing to stretch his wings after a rest that was way too long. He rose into the night's sky. The air was cool and crisp. The call of the Hollow and the glacier was strong. As if his wings had a mind of their own, he didn't even have to think to find his way home. Petolemy was the first to reach the glacier. He looked down on it from the night sky. It looked like a white frozen river with small portals that would allow someone to travel within it freely. He could feel the cold air emanating from the frozen water.

Like fresh water draws salmon during mating season, the glacier was calling him and every one of his kind. The path through the glacier was never the same. Every year it changed.

When navigating the pathway, if the wrong crevasse is chosen, it could lead to a dead end and a head on collision with a wall of solid ice. Though very painful it would not be fatal and the chill of the glacier would speed recovery. Without giving a thought Petolemy folded his wings to his side and plunged straight toward the glacier, just as Seleucid came up from behind him. Seleucid just hovered in midair laughing a joyful laugh of excitement as he too would do the same thing. The wind whistled in Petolemy's ear as he sped toward the ice. Within seconds he disappeared into one of the crevasses. He kept himself focused on both temperature and sight. Where the air was the warmest and the area was the darkest is where he would turn next. After hundreds of years of this he was a master. He turned and twisted through the white and blue frozen maze. He had chosen right and he soon found himself at the opening of the Hollow. Darting inward, he headed to the bottom stopping and hovering in front of the hole leading to the crystal room. He looked up just in time to see Seleucid enter the Hollow. He grinned a friendly grin toward Seleucid. Soon they were both hovering outside the small entrance. "Well," said Seleucid, "are the traps still intact?"

"I don't know," said Petolemy. "I just got here."

Seleucid smiled at Petolemy and said, "There is only one way to find out."

"I know," replied Petolemy, "be my guest."

"Oh, but you are the one who set the traps last year my friend," stated Seleucid.

"How would you know if I had set them right unless you go and inspect my work," said Petolemy.

"Hmm, you do have a point. Very well then," said Seleucid just before he disappeared into the tiny hole, which was almost too small for him to fit through. Suddenly the hall was filled with screams that echoed off the walls as the dust at the bottom of the room was lifted into the air and forced through the tiny hole with a puff. Petolemy's eyes widened as he thought of how these traps were built to end the life of anyone who entered.

"Oh no," found its way out of Petolemy's mouth. He quickly sped through the hole and hovered at the top of the room looking down on the crystal and Seleucid lying at the bottom of the room. He almost thought he had killed him, but he was still in one piece. Just as he realized this, Seleucid cracked an eye open and began to laugh hysterically. Petolemy replied with a smirk and said, "Okay okay, you got me," as he floated slowly down to Seleucid. The smile quickly disappeared from Seleucid's face.

"We were asleep way too long this year Petolemy."

"I know," replied Petolemy. "There must be a way to make it cold and dark all the time, or at least cold." Seleucid smiled a wild crazy smile toward Petolemy. "You have an idea?"

"Yes," replied Seleucid quickly. "But we must first choose the one soul to command the crystal."

"How are we to do that?" asked Petolemy. "No soul wants the power of the crystal less they encounter death at the end of the season."

Seleucid smiled even greater and said, "What if we could promise that the season would never end?"

Seasonal thoughts thickened as the two rooms across from each other were now full of fluttering wings. Conversations about the rumors of a new and existing season filled the rooms. The representatives of each colony were busy asking if there were any souls in their colony that wished to command the stone.

The two rulers of the colonies and guardians of the stone waited with patience while the two representatives informed their colonies and their answer to be returned. Guidian, a rather plump Winged from the colony of Morrigan was the first to make his descent in the shaft. His chubby cheeked face scrunched up and contorted as he attempted to keep himself from falling down the shaft rather than flying down. "Incoming," said Seleucid out of the side of his mouth as he took a sidestep out from underneath Guidian. Guidian seemed to let out a small sigh when he landed in front of Petolemy and Seleucid.

Guidian shook his head with a sad look on his face and said, "No one wants to risk their lives for one season."

The eyes of the colony rulers went from looking grimly at Guidian to looking for hope from above. Just then Modnar, a representative of the colony of Boann, started his descent. A well-formed athletic Winged who needed only to glide down to the bottom. Seleucid looked up and then down in disgust, shaking his head as Modnar slowly made his way down shaking his head in disappointment. "What are we going to do," said Petolemy.

"I haven't the slightest idea," replied Seleucid. Modnar gently landed and took a couple of steps toward Petolemy and Seleucid.

"No way, none of our colony is willing. They all want to know if the rumors are true though," Modnar said.

"Yes," stated Guidian, "everyone is talking about how this season will be different from the rest, but no one really knows."

"Very well," said Seleucid looking the two representatives in the eye. "Go! And tell them all that I have found, a way to bring a permanent darkness to the world and make it colder than ever before."

"We need a strong and brave commander who is not afraid to take chances, who is willing to bring an end to the reign of the sun so that we no longer have to hide from it. And who is willing to bring an end to all the seasons," Petolemy said. Modnar looked at Seleucid and Petolemy and nodded before effortlessly rising up to his colony. Guidian sighed as he looked up, scrunched up his eyes, and proceeded to rise slowly up the shaft.

Seleucid laughed and said, "We should bring him along the journey for morale."

"Well at least he would lose some weight," replied Petolemy with a smile on his face. Seleucid agreed with a chuckle.

Guidian slowly made his appearance up over and on to the ledge of the colony of Morrigan. His eyes squinting and his fist clenched. The loud room of talkative brothers and sisters became silent when they saw Guidian. "Well," said Dameron assistant to Guidian, "is it true?"

Guidian took a big breath and shouted, "A new season is now upon us. So now we must find a new commander of the stone. One who will lead us all into a world of frozen darkness forever and bring an end to the seasons. Who among you is willing? Step forward now."

Dameron came forward, "I will represent." Dameron turned to face the crowd. He stood taller than most and had a great booming voice.

"Is there anyone that will oppose?" yelled Guidian.

"I challenge," was shouted from the back of the colony. A tall slender Winged flew up and over the crowd, landing in front of Guidian, then turning to face the large Dameron who gave a long hard look with his intimidating battle-scared face at his tall, slender, less intimidating foe.

"What is your name brother?" asked Dameron. A moment passed and no reply came from his opponent. He just stood there with a blank look, staring him in the face. Dameron was an honored warrior and did not have the patience for games, especially from the likes of this Winged. He took a short moment to study his long slender face with sunken cheeks and eyes that seemed not to focus. Dameron leaned forward a bit, and his hand came shooting out to push his opponent in the shoulder. His hand was soon held by another hand, Dameron found himself caught off balance and being pulled forward. His opponent quickly stepped aside to allow Dameron to fall forward toward Guidian.

Guidian's eyes widened and he too stepped aside with speed he did not know he had. Dameron found himself staring down the great shaft as the ice flow above cracked loudly echoing down the shaft. His wings beating quite fast he just hovered there wallowing in his own stupidity. A few chuckles could be heard in the crowd. His opponent did not think it was funny, however.

Dameron's wings brought him upright and he spun around to look at that face. Blank, without the least bit of emotion, and eyes like puddles of blood in the light of a full moon. He knew he had to watch himself. He flew rapidly toward his opponent and stopped only a foot away from him. But there wasn't a sign of any recognition. Almost as if he was dead. He just seemed to stare of into nothingness. The dance began and Dameron was the lead. With every move he made it was countered. There were no offensive moves made by his opponent, and no blows landed by Dameron. He was just too fast, and he knew what was happening. He knew he was starting to wear down. *How could he keep up like this*, Dameron thought to himself. He knew he was being toyed with. He tried to take it to the air by flying up, but his opponent stayed on the ground waiting for him to come back. Never challenging, just waiting for his next move. He had to think of something. It came to him that he would try the same thing his opponent was doing. So, he flew down to him just a foot away and stared with a blank stare into the face of his opponent. It was like a painful staring contest. Dameron tried to find his reflection in the eyes of his opponent but there was no reflection. They seemed to absorb everything in front of them. Dameron started to feel like the room was spinning around. He laughed just before he found himself face first on the ground. He came to with both arms behind his back and pressure on his back from the weight of his opponent. "Do you yield?" came a deep whisper in his ear.

"Yes." cried Dameron. "I yield, just tell me what your name is."

"Bob," announced the voice in his ear.

"Bob?" repeated Dameron. A low chuckle started deep in Dameron as he rolled Bob off of him. On his back he broke out into full laughter. He could barely bring himself to his feet. Hands on his knees he stood before Bob in hysterics. He took Bob by the hand and shook it. "Bob it is then," announced Dameron as he hugged the bewildered Bob.

Modnar rose from the depths of the shaft-like fog rolling over a hill at midnight, cold, quiet, and without consciousness. His mind was abuzz about the things he would like to do if he could command the stone. He hovered there over the colony of Boann watching all of the people in the colony talking among themselves totally oblivious to the fact that he had just arrived. *Look at them,* he thought to himself. *Year after year they come here to squabble and live out their endless dull lives.*

One by one they began to notice him floating there looking at them like a scientist studying his subjects. The noise of the colony slowly dimmed to silence, "I wish to challenge for the stone," he roared. "There is a new season awing, there are plans that might extend the season for a long time if not forever. I am tired of going season after season without end. I am willing to take the chance. Who must I challenge for the right?" Modnar began to pace, his voice starting very low, "Nights far gone and never last." Then louder, "The stars never change with time gone past." Louder still, "We spin within as planets stroll by. I wish to fly in the never-ending night sky." He stopped, turned, and roared like a hungry beast, "Who will challenge me?" Every muscle in his body flexed with his fists clenched and at his side. But the only thing that could be heard was the sound of laughter coming from the other room across the shaft.

Dameron's laughter slowly came under control as he began to hear a voice coming from across the shaft. It started low and grew louder. "All you children that fear the light, brothers, sisters, you're all dead inside. Hide from the sun in your slumber of death. Only to awake like living dead, I say to you that I will stop the light. I will take the stone and open my third eye. Forever I will hold the power." Modnar now had his hand stretched out before him and his eyes gazing at his clenched fist.

Dameron, like everyone else, had focused his full attention on Modnar. Dameron shifted his attention every now and then at Bob who had an emotionless gaze set on Modnar. And just as Modnar finished his speech, Dameron suddenly lost control of his breathing and a huge puff of air forced its way out of Dameron's closed mouth with a few drops of spittle. His eyes watered and he took in a huge gulp of air and began laughing uncontrollably. His arm stretched out and pointing a shaking finger at Modnar. Modnar squinted his eyes at Dameron and descended into the depths of the shaft to confront Petolemy and Seleucid.

Bob looked at Dameron and said, "Are you coming Dameron?"

"What, with you?" he replied.

"Yes! You do realize that since you lost to me you are now indebted to me as my servant if I should win possession of the stone." Dameron's mouth dropped open and his gazed turned to Guidian for confirmation and some support. Guidian had his hand over his mouth to cover the grin on his face, but Dameron could see his pudgy cheeks were all red.

"Yabe," said Dameron. He turned to look at Bob, but he was already gone. Dameron sighed and dropped down the shaft.

Modnar was standing before Petolemy telling him how no one from the colony of Boann was willing to challenge him for the fight for the stone. Seleucid was looking up and said, "There is however someone from the colony of Morrigan that looks more than willing to challenge you for the stone." Modnar turned and looked up to see Dameron and Bob descending down the shaft.

"Why are two of them coming down?" Boann stated that whoever challenges and loses becomes the servant of the winner. So, if I win this fight, I get both of them as my servant?" asked Modnar.

"Yes," replied Petolemy. "But if you lose you will become the third servant of whoever you are fighting. *Hmmm*, Modnar thought to himself.

"I suppose the one that was pointing his finger at me and laughing is the one that I will be fighting. He looks like an easy opponent. He will pay dearly for his stupidity." Dameron landed first in front of Seleucid and Bob quickly landed behind Dameron.

"We will be representing the colony of Morrigan," stated Dameron.

Modnar looked at them and then at Petolemy. "What does he mean we?" Seleucid looked at Modnar.

"It's quite simple Modnar; here we have master and servant. They will be fighting together against their opponent." Modnar realized his arrogance as Seleucid went on to explain in greater detail what Petolemy had said earlier.

"But which one of you is master and which is servant?" asked Modnar.

"Does it really matter Modnar?" asked Dameron. Bob remained silent.

"But this isn't fair," stated Modnar, "two against one."

"Very well then," said Bob in his deep voice. "I will stand aside so that it will be fair." Dameron's jaw dropped open as he looked up at

Bob. Bob's emotionless face looked down on Dameron as a lightning-fast wink was given to Dameron as a token of assurance.

Dameron smiled, "Very well then. It looks like it's just you and me Modnar."

Modnar smiled in approval. *"Baka yamero yo! Chibi!"* came out of Modnar with a slow and sarcastic drawl, thinking that Dameron was not as worldly or experienced as he.

But his pride was extinguished when Dameron countered with low growl of, *"kono Kusottare."*

Their conversation was interrupted with the sound of metal objects hitting the ground, which was immediately followed by the sound of the glacier overhead cracking like thunder as if to answer the call of metal. Seleucid and Petolemy had thrown down two hay baler hooks. Dameron suddenly was filled with memories of when he first had to fight with hay baler hooks. Blood flowed like wine in a French whore colony. He had survived but he had to bury himself in permafrost for months. Modnar also was familiar with large hooks but not like these. He felt confident though and was thinking that this should be fun. "First to yield, loses," stated Seleucid.

Both Dameron and Modnar dove for the hooks. Dameron was first to reach his and tucked into a roll and stood up behind Modnar who had landed on his stomach, arm stretched out and holding the hook. Dameron turned around to see Modnar on his knees getting up off the ground. He ran straight for Modnar, hook held high in the air. Modnar knew he was coming and gave Dameron a back kick right in the chest like a mule. It knocked the air out of Dameron and sent him back a few feet. Enough time for Modnar to get to his feet, turn around, and face Dameron. Each of them was standing no more than four or five feet apart from each other. Their eyes locked together as if in a staring contest and the first one that blinked would get an ice pick in the side of the neck. Each one of them began to feel their way around to find their center of gravity for better balance. Fortunately, Dameron's stance was low, which allowed him to be already at his center of gravity. Modnar slowly began to bend his knees to get lower to the ground. But was not quick enough as Dameron shot his pick straight up and latched on to Modnar's pick. Caught by surprise Modnar stood up and pulled back on his pick as Dameron jumped toward him. Swinging his feet in front of him, Dameron planted his feet firmly in the chest of Modnar, sending him over backward and on to the ground, followed with the weight of Dameron crashing down on his chest. A strange wheezing sound came out of Modnar as the last bit of air was crushed out of his lungs. Dameron pulled hard on Modnar's pick and yanked it right out of his hand and sent it flying behind him, with the sound of ringing steel. Petolemy and Morrigan both took a sidestep away from each other as the ice pick flew between them and against the wall. Dameron came down on his knees straddling the neck of Modnar whose face was turning blue. "Dameron would you get off him so he can yield," said Bob in a calm yet firm tone.

"Ha-ha!" announced Dameron, "Didn't see that coming did ya." As he rose, he turned to Bob and gave him a wink of his own.

"Impressive," stated Bob. Bob sighed, "What am I to do with you two?"

"Well," said Morrigan, "you can start by coming with us. We have lots to discuss. You can leave these two to themselves, I don't think they will be going anywhere." Petolemy looked down on Dameron and Modnar and bestowed upon them the look of death, which made the mere thought of leaving vanish from their minds.

"We have much to discuss," stated Morrigan as he reached down and put his hand on Bob's shoulder. They began to walk slowly toward the hole in the wall that led to the stone. Petolemy followed close behind Morrigan and Bob. Bob could feel the eyes of Petolemy looking down on him. "Before we give you the stone, we must tell you about it and what it does. We must also inform you of your mission. We think we have found a way to bring many years of darkness upon the world and maybe forever. With this darkness comes the ice and snow that would get rid of the seasons and allow us to move about without having to hibernate."

"Listen," said Petolemy. "You cannot travel in darkness though. To know the way, you must have the light."

"How will I travel in the light?" asked Bob. "If I travel in the light I will die." Almost in unison a rumble of laughter came from deep within Morrigan and Petolemy.

"Yes, you will die, but then live forever," Petolemy and Morrigan looked up at the hole in the side of the shaft and flew up and in the hole. Bob followed close behind.

"Did you hear that," stated Modnar, "they're going to kill Bob." Dameron looked up at the hole in the wall.

"Hmmm, doesn't sound like he is going to die. He has a mission to do and guess what, we're going to be his minions."

"Yea, well I'm nobody's subordinate," growled Modnar.

"That may be, but it sounds like we are in for a lot of fun and adventure."

The room was dark even to Bob, whose eyes could see in the dead of night like it was the day. The only light that could be seen was the slight ray of light coming from the entrance to the room. Dust swirling around in the room revealed it to him. But the darkness cut it off and seemed to swallow the small ray until it was gone. He could hear the men's voices down below. "Hello," he said. "Where are you guys?"

"Can't you see?" they replied.

"I cannot, it is too dark."

"You must listen," they said. They began to tell the story of how before the foundation of the planet they were created. They told of how they were to do the work of the one who had created them, and as they went on with their story, he began to see a slight glow in the center of the room. They told of how they would always walk in darkness unless their ears can hear so that they may receive sight and see the light. The stone grew brighter and brighter showing almost the whole room. By the end of the story the whole room was lit up. He marveled at the bright stone, supported by the intertwining wooden tree that looked as old as time itself.

"What is that?" gasped Bob.

"It is the light through which all things may be accomplished," stated Petolemy.

"Can I touch it?" asked Bob.

"If you touch it that means you accept it," stated Morrigan.

"And if you accept it and fail in your mission, when the seasons change you may not be able to survive the separation from it." Bob looked at Morrigan and then at Petolemy He smiled and an uncontrollable shot of air came out of Bob's nose, almost like a giddy little boy. He looked at the stone and then flew quickly toward it. He only stopped in mid-flight in front of the stone for a second and quickly seized it. He held it in his hands and gazed deeply into it. He seemed to feel as if he was bonding with it, becoming attached, as if now it knew what he was thinking and out of realizing what had just taken place, he let go of it in fear and amazement. He then realized he was not of this world. None of them were of this world. The light went out as it fell to the ground. The room was filled with laughter as Morrigan and Petolemy watched and remembered how they too did the same thing when they first held the stone. Bob blushed upon knowing that he had never had such a close relationship with anything or anyone until now.

"Why are we here?" asked Bob. The laughter left the room leaving only an echo as if someone was mocking the question. "Does anyone else know that we are not of this world?" asked Bob.

"Only the ones who survive the separation from the stone know," stated Morrigan.

"But why? We should tell everyone."

Petolimy sighed, "Only those that have an ear will hear and only those that have eyes will see the light."

"You could not see the light until you had ears and heard our story."

"You were chosen to hear so you saw the light."

"Not everyone is chosen, and so not everyone will hear." Morrigan flew up close to Bob. "You are now in an important position and must not be mocked. There will be a time to tell all but at this time I'm not sure that everyone is ready to hear it all."

Modnar and Dameron sat at the bottom of the shaft waiting. "How long are we supposed to wait for?" asked Modnar.

"Well, I suppose until they come out," answered Dameron, in a smooth insulting tone.

"So Dameron, tell me, how do you feel about your situation?"

"What situation?" he replied.

"The fact that you lost to Bob in a battle, only to become his slave."

"I am nobody's slave," replied Dameron.

"What are you then?"

"I'm one link in a chain of command. One link below Bob and one link above you. So mind your tongue."

"Hmmm," replied Modnar. "So, what do you think of your one link above you?"

"I'm not sure, but there is something about him. I would advise to try and stay on his good side."

"Look," said Dameron as he pointed to the hole in the shaft. Petolemy and Morrigan emerged from the hole and flew straight up and out of the shaft. Bob soon appeared and looked down at Modnar and Dameron.

"Go to your dens, it is almost light. We will meet here when it is again dark."

"Aye," replied Dameron and Modnar.

Bob's flight was lost to him and his wings carried him home as if they had a mind of their own. His thoughts drifted off to the events that had happened this night. Like a quill writing in an ancient tongue on his forehead the thoughts came to him. "How souless am I. Never dying, yet dead. I almost wish for death if I should part from this stone. Maybe then I will find that I have a soul after all. What ancient nemesis has come upon me that I should live in darkness yet walk in the light."

Digging through the frozen soil, the tundra mole, a small, sight-challenged rodent perseveres, slowly burrowing its way through the arctic wasteland emitting slow grating scratching sounds as it burrowed its way through the tundra. It was nighttime and it was extending its tunnel that it used to store food so that it may spend the winter in it. It was getting close to Bobs den and the sound soon entered his dreams. He was hovering high over a mountain top, higher than he had ever been before. It was no longer cold, there was light all around but the sun was not out. A giant monster was roaring. It held a whip of fire and was lashing at him with every scraping sound he heard. The sky then began to shake and rocks were falling on his head as the mole broke through his den. He awoke sharply and screamed as a black furry nose started to sniff at him. The mole let out a sharp squeal like a stuck pig and bolted in the other direction. Bob then slumped down in his wrecked den. "Damn moles," he said out loud. He began to think back to the previous evening and what he had to do. A swift wind blew across the ground. It was a clear crisp night. Moonlight was bouncing off of the snow crystals like little sparkling diamonds all over the ground. Bob emerged from his den. The wind blew back his hair as he raised his nose in the air and smelled the surrounding area. The cold always kept the air fresh and clean. This time though there was a warm smell coming from up wind. The stench of animal smell made his nose crinkle. This animal was only admitting a very low amount of heat so it couldn't be that big.

Though the smell repulsed him, he has been known to have some fun with some animals, that is, if they couldn't fly. He stretched his wings back and let the wind push them together. He wrapped the tips of wings one inside another and flexed his back muscles, cracking all his wing joints with a sound of a crackling campfire. He tilted his head back and rolled it around his shoulders. He stuck out his hands and shook the sleep off. He smelled the air again and tried to figure out what kind of animal was out there. It had moved from its previous position but not far. He reached into his pocket and fumbled with the stone that he had received last night. He then noticed two glowing orbs in the distance. Not far off and still upwind. They shifted back and forth as if they were looking for something. They then turned away as the animal started to slowly walk away. Bob let the wind catch his wings and he slowly rose into the air. It was when he was about twice the height of the animal that he figured out that it was an arctic fox. He let his body become parallel to the ground and then aimed for the fox and started his descent straight in on the fox.

He came down along the right side of the fox and matched its speed and direction and then up and directly over the fox and then landed right behind the fox's neck. He grabbed onto two big clumps of hair and pulled back on them. The fox jumped straight into the air. Its ears flattened as it came down. Bob cheered and began to laugh until the fox rolled on its back and proceeded to grind Bob into the snow. Bob was still holding on for dear life due to the fact that it had just recently snowed a few feet of soft powder that day. The fox's legs moved about aimlessly in the air as it wiggled its body about in the snow. It then came to its feet as Bob spit out a mouthful of snow. It then bolted toward a grove of trees. Bob was about to depart seeing the direction the fox was taking, when a window began to open up in his mind. The fox had vanished and snow was moving rapidly underneath him, but he was not running. He saw the woods coming closer and closer. He looked to the right of the woods and then noticed he was moving parallel to the forest. The fox had begun to slow down and eventually stopped. It sat down in the snow breathing heavily from the run. Bob began laughing so hard he almost fell off the fox. As soon as Bob left the animal it regained its self-control. The smell of a dead animal in the distance overpowered its senses and it took off in the direction of a fresh kill.

Bob realized what he had to do so he followed the animal to a carcass of a partially eaten moose in the midst of a sea of blood-drenched snow. He waited till the animal had its fill of the rotting corpse. As soon as it left he flew over to what was left of the moose. A piece of hide that had been stripped clean of its meat laid in the midst of gnawed bone and tangled intestines. Taking a deep breath he flew down and snatched it up much like an eagle swooping down and plucking a salmon out of the water. Finding the closest large chunk of ice he glided down. Grabbing the fur side of the hide he began grinding the hide into the jagged surfaces of the ice, rendering it clean of any meat. There were several long tufts of fur almost like hair on the hide. he cut them free from the hide and flipped the hide over. he put the stone in the center of the hide and brought all the ends together. Taking a couple of the hairs Bob tied the ends together making a pouch and then a long loop with the remaining hairs secured to the pouch. The loop was too large for Bob so he had to double tie it up a few times so that it could fit around his neck like a charm. Taking to the air again he was glad to be away from the warm fleshy creatures. But he knew that this had great potential and would play a major role in what he had to accomplish. Rising above the trees he felt almost happy in a mischievous kind of way. He began to think of Dameron and Modnar. He was thinking of the amount of distance they would have to cover and how it would be very tiring. There must be an easier way of traveling, he thought to himself. As he looked down on the trees he saw how white everything was. There was almost no way to tell where the trees ended and the snow began. He then noticed a very dark circle in the midst of the snow-covered trees. "Could it be," he thought to himself as he glided down for a closer look. Sure enough there was a little white snowball in the center, which could only be the head of a bald eagle. This would be the ultimate mode of travel around these parts, he thought. This would prove to be very dangerous as well. He began a slow spiraling descent above the eagle. He did not want to catch the eye of an eagle. Though he would prove to be nothing more than a small snack, and he could most likely outmaneuver the huge bird, he did not want it to move. As he got closer he noticed that the eagle was finishing up a meal. It seemed to be having a bit of a time swallowing its kill whole. A patch of well-matted fur was sticking out of its mouth, which seemed to have a couple of legs and talon feet attached. It started to bend its head down as it brought up one of its feet and grabbed the feet of its prey, ripping it in half. Bob's heart fainted when the eagle lifted his head up toward the sky. The eagle opened its mouth to let the dead carcass slide down its throat. Bob sighed in relief when he noticed its eyes were closed. When the eagle looked down at the second part of its meal Bob seized the moment taking off the necklace and diving in on the back of the neck of the eagle. Holding on to the sack that held the stone he whipped the line around the eagle's neck like a lasso. Holding on tight to the loop just above where it was tied to the pouch he landed with a poof on the feathery neck of the eagle. The next thing he saw in his mind was the lower half of a bloody bird at his feet.

Modnar and Dameron were in the great hall awaiting Bob's return. The great hall was empty. All the other Winged were off on their adventures for the season. A walrus tusk hung from the ceiling by a strip of tooled mammoth hide, which was split into two three-foot-long strips just below the tusk and then anchored to Modnar and Dameron's wrists. The tusk was spinning rapidly. A hole was drilled through the center of the tusk so that as it spun the hole would flash by each person. Modnar and Dameron took turns trying to thread their spear through the hole with short jabs. The one who was first to complete this won. They stood close to the spinning tusk each one trying to keep it from moving away from them with the anchor in their left hand. Their spears missing their mark would sometimes come close to hitting the other opponent if he was standing too close. Sometimes cursing would ring out accusing the other of missing on purpose just to get a chance to strike the other. But they both knew that this was not the case, for the wager on this game was too high. The only other sound that could be heard was the shuffling of feet and the clicking sound as the spears struck the bone. Modnar lunged forward toward the tusk with his spear giving slack to the anchor and Dameron pulled on his anchor moving the tusk away from Modnar but closer to him. Dameron had to adjust and move forward to strike the tusk causing him to miss and go past the tusk and strike Modnar. He pulled back quick enough though, so it did not pierce through the clothing of Modnar. "Hey," said Modnar. "Watch it."

"Well, don't pull it so close to you," said Dameron.

"Well, if you would keep your anchor taut it wouldn't happen." The tusk was slowly being chipped away to nothing. Each strike on the tusk took a chip out of the bone until finally the tusk cracked in half. Realizing that the game was a draw, Modnar spun his spear around to the blunt end and cracked it over the head of Dameron breaking the spear in half. Dameron staggered back and glared back at Modnar. Dameron began to take jabs at Modnar with his spear. All Modnar could do was make small parries with his now very short spear. The sound of clinking steal echoed down the shaft. Modnar's short spear was finally knocked out of his hand and to the floor. Dameron drew his spear back and was getting ready to throw it with all his might. Modnar began to take to the air. Dameron began to throw his spear but Bob had grabbed it just as he was about to throw. His hand slid down the shaft of the spear by the force of his throw. His hand didn't stop until it hit the backward facing spikes of the spear's arrowhead. A loud cry could be heard echoing throughout the great hall, as Dameron grabbed his hand in pain. Bob now had the blunt end of the spear in his hand. He flipped it in the air and grabbed the spear just above the spear head and cracked the blunt end of the spear over Dameron's head. Dameron passed out and fell to the ground.

"You didn't have to knock him out Bob."

"I know, but I just couldn't stand to see him in pain," they both looked at each other and began to laugh. Dameron's eyes slowly began to open.

Everything was a blur to him. His eyes slowly began to focus and see two faces looking down on him. "Why did you have to go and do that?" asked Dameron.

"Well, it looked like you were about to kill Modnar."

"Naw," said Dameron as he rose to his feet rubbing his head, "we were just playing."

"So what do we have planned for this evening?"

"We need to harvest guano," stated Bob.

"Guano?" asked Modnar with one eyebrow scrunched down on one eye and the other eyebrow rose up over the other.

"What kind of guano?" asked Dameron in a kind of stern voice.

"Bat guano," answered Bob with a half-smile on his face.

"Eeeewwww," stated Modnar. "What are we going to do with that?"

"Saltpeter," said Dameron. "We are going to make Saltpeter aren't we?"

"Mmmhmm," came the reply.

"I hate bats," stated Modnar in a low grumble.

"This time of year, the bats are out of their caves moving toward a warmer climate so you won't have to worry about encountering any," said Bob. "But there is one encounter you will have to face." Both Dameron and Modnar stood there silently looking at Bob waiting for him to tell them what was going on. Both their eyes opened wide as Bob grinned a grin that no one should ever reveal. An oily blackness torn from murder darkened the shiny white backdrop behind Bob. The wind generated by its flight blew Bob's long hair in front of him. He began to laugh uncontrollably as both Modnar and Dameron began to faint. Before they could hit the floor they were plucked up by sharp black talons and flown out of the den. Weaving in and out of the crevasse within the glacier, a path well memorized by Bob, they soon found themselves awakening limp and thousands of feet above grown. The night was clear, cold and dry, drier than any desert. Down below most of the trees were incased in a thin layer of ice surrounding the leafless limbs making them look like shiny albino trees. It was so quiet except for the sound of beating wings. Dameron began to enjoy the free ride to wherever they were going but Modnar began to feel betrayed and kidnapped.

They flew over miles of rugged glacial fiords and channels. Ancient frozen forests on islands within rivers of ice, filled with deer, bear and eagles. The pristine beauty lay stretched out before them as far as they could see, divided only by mountain glaciers. Their destination soon appeared in the distance. Its dark peaks poking up over earth's curvature.

Their destination was a huge mountain, which looked like it was once a large round mountainous range of solid rock. Now it looked as if God himself took a giant sword and sliced it into many slices, which fell inward toward the center piece on both sides, making it a tall, pointed mountain with many plates of jagged rock so steep that not even snow was capable of resting on it. The snow fell and was channeled down between the plates, accumulating at the bottom like sand at the bottom of an hourglass. Each space between the slices of rock had its own cone of snow pointing its way to the top of the mountain. Inside the mountain was a giant cave. The cave had two openings—one was guarded by a frozen waterfall and the other was a steam vent for one of the nearby volcanoes. Rather than risking being exposed to heat they opted for the frozen ice. The ice covering the cave opening was clear and polished by the wind. Just on the other side of the icy door was the skeleton of an ancient blue whale. Its mouth open wide as if it was about to take a bite out of something. They were all drained of energy from the long trip and needed to recharge. They all laid their hands on the ice at the same time. The ice clouded over and began to change colors. As the impact of the starving group started to have its toll on the ice, it slowly began to change colors. The color changes stopped on a fowl green. When they were done feeding on the ice, the cave entrance gave the whales mouth the illusion of having nasty green teeth as it shattered into jagged edges. The temperature of the cave was a bit warmer than the outside but it was cold enough to keep things frozen in the cave entrance. A rush of cold wind came from their backs and into the cave, relieving them of the wretched damp smell of warm drying guano. As they walked through the skeletal atrium of whale bones the wind whipped through the tunnel. The bones moaned as if the whale was giving its last protest against their trespassing. Their jaws had dropped heavily as they walked within the long skeleton. Bones of the skeleton were incased in ice. The ice reflected their image as they walked past each bone. It was like a cylindered mirror and between each bone was a blackened void. As they approached a rib bone their image would appear from the void getting bigger and bigger until they reached the center of the bone when there reflected image would be the same size as they were. As they ventured pass the bone their image began to shrink again and disappear into the black void until they approached another rib bone.

On the floor laid loose shale. Small clinking sounds came from the floor as they walked on the stones. It got warmer as they ventured deeper in the cave and the smell of guano had gone unnoticed until they stepped in something that went crackle then squish instead of clink. "Mmm guano," said Bob. "Apparently the bats have been living in this area," stated Bob. There was a dry white crust of guano on the surface and an icky squishy filling.

Their steps were out of sync just enough to where they could hear every icky squishy step they took; the ground became solid again as they ventured on through the cave. Bob stopped walking and looked to the ground. The remains of four creatures lay on the ground. Their skins were removed and laid only a few feet away. There were two human remains as well. Bob almost felt jealous of these people. To have it all come to an end. It would be so relaxing. Bob grabbed a skull of one of the animals and hugged it with a loving affection of their passing. To finally leave this world, pass on to the next, and be home again would be so nice. A small tear ran down Bob's cheek. Dameron and Modnar stared a worried stare at Bob. A new fear was now instilled in them as they both whispered as if talking to themselves, "Necro." Bob's eyes wandered to Dameron and Modnar. He composed himself and threw the skull to Dameron who snapped to and received the skull to his chest. Bob picked up another one and threw it at Modnar.

"Here, fill these with the top layer of guano." Bob walked over to the hides that lay next to the bones of the animals and cut a large square shaped piece and filled it with guano. Bob looking around noticed that there was what looked like the remains of a fire pit amidst the bodies. He walked over the fire pit filled only with dried ash and dumped his share of the dried-up crusty guano into the fire pit. Dameron and Modnar followed suit. Taking one of the small bones of one of the animals Bob began to mix the guano with the ashes. After Bob was done Dameron and Modnar put some of the mixture into the skulls and began to slowly grind it with stones they had found in the cave. When they were done they would dump the powder into the sack that Bob had made with the animal skin. The sun rose and set many times before they were done grinding the powder finer and finer.

The smell of sulfur was heavy in the cave. They all stood above the sack of potassium nitrate. A cool breeze came from the mouth of the wale, passed through them and went toward the opening at the top of the mountain. They tilted their heads up like cats sniffing the air. At that same instant their eyes focused on the sealing of the cave and noticed some kind of writing or drawing. Clicking sounds came from deep within the cave. The reason for the demise of the creatures whose bones lay scattered among them never entered their minds until now. The same thing that instilled fear into Dameron and Modnar gave Bob a sense of relief and an answer to the question of how to obtain sulfur from deep within the cave without getting too close to the heat of the volcano. Bob looked down to his side and reached into the pouch that contained the stone. Taking the line attached to the stone out first he made many loops out of it and hung it around his neck. The clicking sounds of a Giant Meta Bourneti came closer and closer from within the cave. Its fat round body glistened with black oily secretions. Both above and below the spider's body was a purple ring in which it kept its venom. Small purple veins ran from the circles to the small head in front of the fat body, keeping a supply of the venom running to its mouth like saliva. There were two pincers that proceeded out of its mouth that would hold its prey while its piercing tongue would penetrate the victim's body like a needle and suck the contents out. Its body was supported by four legs on each side. Each of the legs went up from the body at a forty-five-degree angle well above the body and then down again at a steeper angle to the ground. Each of the legs was covered in a spiky shell like a dungeness crab. Its shell made a clicking like sound when its end feet hit the cave floor.

Both Modnar and Dameron looked toward Bob as his gaze turned in the direction of the sounds that came down from the tunnel. The cave floor disappeared only five yards away as it became a descent deeper into the earth. Bob was the first to start making his way down the cave, followed by Modnar and Dameron. The cave floor soon leveled out. Louder and louder the sound became until from within the cave beyond their sight came a stream of spider web. All three of them fell to the floor as stream after stream of spider web was shot out. Sometimes a long steady stream, as if the spider was trying to capture them and wrap them up in a cocoon. As soon as the assault started it had stopped. There was an eerie silence. No sound of movement or anything came from the spider. They stood up and looked behind them. A giant sticky spider trap covered the way out of the tunnel like a giant sticky wall that dripped with spider goo. They then turned slowly to the direction from which the spider was now approaching. The first thing to come into view was the two front legs as they came forward pulling itself forward.

Dameron and Modnar stood in awe as the head came into view, its pincers looking like two giant black claws dripping with its venom were imbedded with curved needle-like teeth surrounded by lips that were like black rubber that quivered ever so slightly. It had four eyes in the center of its head. They looked almost like two sets of human eyes. Like it had taken part human form after sucking them out of the skull. The rest of its body followed and it seemed like the veins that flowed with venom were pulsating with anticipation of its next victim. It emitted a kind of cooing or purring sound. It was almost relaxing to hear. But from beyond the spider and on the cave floor came an almost liquid mist. It was only inches thick and it slowly made its way underneath the spider and moved past it and toward Bob, Dameron, and Modnar. They followed it with their eyes. Soon it was around their feet. It felt cold and relaxing to them, almost enjoyable. Bob, taking no chances, rose into the air. He watched the spider's eyes as they followed him into the air. Bob could hear screams coming from Modnar and Dameron as they rose into the air. They both had several smaller spiders attached to their feet sucking their blood like oversized mosquitoes. The mother spider focused her attention on them as screeching sounds came from the small critters as they were being kicked off their victim's feet. The mother spider dipped her head to the floor as its abdomen rose. A stream of spider web shot out and grabbed Modnar. Modnar began flying backward as the spider pulled on the web bringing Modnar slowly closer and closer to the pincers dripping with poison. He grabbed the tugging web with his hands only to find himself securely attached to it. Dameron offered no assistance as he looked down at the mist waiting for more of those little creatures to launch themselves at him.

Bob took this chance and flew around behind the spider. The upper set of eyes followed him while the other two concentrated on its prey. The giant pinchers cut the web holding Modnar and then grabbed it again with its two front feet. Dameron looked up from the floor of the cave and at Modnar. Cursing he knew that if he didn't do something he would have hell to pay, so he flew over and grabbed Modnar. A tug of war began between Modnar, Dameron, and the spider. The spider whipped at Bob with the remaining length of web it had attached to its abdomen. Bob had the line attached to the stone and was whirling it around like a lasso. He was taking aim for the neck of the spider when the web smacked Bob right in the chest. Bob let the noose fly. The spider jerked hard on the web pulling Bob quickly toward its pinchers. Bob, along with the noose, were hurling toward the spider's head and pinchers. The loop of the line hit the spider in the back of the neck and looped around the pinchers just as the spider was closing them to crush Bob between them. The web was loose but still attached to Bob. Bob spread out his wings and began to fly upward and away from the pinchers pulling hard on the line he held in his hand. His flight was cut short as the tension in the spider web he had attached to his chest became taut. It acted like a rubber band as Bob flew up it and stretched it a foot or so before it snapped back, sending him hurling down toward the spider. Bob came down hard on the spider's fat abdomen. The spider let loose a loud squeal like a stuck pig. The impact caused the spider to let loose the line it had been pulling on and both Modnar and Dameron went flying backward and into the sticky web wall the spider had created. Bob sank down slightly as the spider's skin gave way to the impact and then, returning to its shape, bounced Bob ever so slightly up and then down again. Bob held tight, however, to the line in his hand. The spider became very still as four windows opened up in Bob's mind. Bob screamed as his mind tried to comprehend and control four independent windows. The cave was swirling around him and he started to become nauseas. Before he could get one eye under control he coughed up a white milky substance. Modnar and Dameron just looked on at the spider in amazement as the four eyes were all twirling around. Like a slot machine spinning around first one eye clicked into place then another and another until the fourth one snapped into position. The mist that covered the cave floor retreated back and down the tunnel. Bob sat on the abdomen of the spider, the end of the line, with the stone in his hand. Bob began to feel sluggish as the warmth the spider's body was generating was a little overwhelmin for Bob. He quickly dismounted the spider and walked over to the wall that held Modnar and Dameron. Sitting on the ground a few feet in front of the wall he put his head down and closed his eyes. He knew that getting used to maneuvering the spider with four eyes would take some getting used to. Modnar and Dameron struggled to free themselves from the web, but found their efforts useless. The only way out would be to have Bob's spider cut them loose. Bob, with his head in his hands, focused on Modnar and Dameron. Dameron's head was slightly above Modnar's head as they both were frozen still in anticipation of the spider's approach. Dameron's attention was so intensely concentrated on the spider as it approached, with its giant pinchers, horrible needle-like teeth, and quivering lips, that he didn't notice when drool started to drip out of the side of his mouth and onto Modnar. "Hey," shouted Modnar, snapping Dameron out of his trance.

"Sorry," said Dameron. Keeping his eyes focused on the spider. The spider seemed to move in almost a robot fashion. First the right front leg would move forward followed by the second right leg and third. The fourth right leg would push forward as the left side would start the same cycle and the right front would come down followed by the second and third. Slowly the spider began to move in a more fluid motion. Soon Bob found out that he could blink the eyes of the spider and learned how to close two eyes, which made it easier to see in his point of view. The sweat began to poor off of Modnar and Dameron. Dameron's sweat began to drip off him and onto Modnar.

"Hey," shouted Modnar.

"I can't help it," said Dameron, "it's coming right for us."

"Bob is controlling it Dameron."

"I know but still, look at those teeth and those lips."

"Okay, you do have a point there, just try and calm down a bit." The spider slowly came closer and closer to Modnar and Dameron. The horrified look on them made Bob smile. Unfortunately, that made the spider smile as well, which in turn creeped out the two victims even more. Bob couldn't hold back any longer. With his head in his hands, looking down while he sat on the ground, he began to laugh. It was quiet at first. The spider stopped and its smile got even bigger with its needle teeth gleaming in the darkness. The whole spider began to shake as Bob began to laugh harder; a shrieking sound came from it in unison with Bob's outward burst of laughter. The spectacle was so hideous that Modnar and Dameron began to scream. Tears started coming out of all four eyes of the spider as Bob completely lost it. Bob wasn't able to gain composure until Modnar and Dameron had passed out in either fear or disgust, which Bob did not know.

Bob began to maneuver the spider in front of them. Starting above Dameron, Bob began cutting along the top with the pinchers. The spider's saliva dripping with poison ran down the pinchers and onto the web. It began to dissolve the web. The spider then began to cut down the sides until a nice square was cut and they both received a rude awakening when they both hit the floor face first.

Their backs began to smoke as the acid from the spider's saliva began to eat away at the web attached to them. They both began to curse as they rolled around on the ground trying to get the poisonous spider saliva off of them. Bob stood up and walked over to them and helped them up. "I don't see how using this spider is going to help us," said Modnar.

"We will use it to gather the sulfur for us," stated Bob. "It will take all my concentration, but I can maneuver the spider down into the area closest to the volcano opening through the steam vents where we can't go."

"Can I count on you two to watch my back while I do this?"

"Aye," said both Modnar and Dameron at the same time.

"Very well then," I will sit here, close my eyes, and try not to make any sound while I concentrate on this spider."

Bob sat on the floor legs crossed and eyes closed. The spider closed two of its eyes and spun around. The giant spider made the tunnel feel small. The darkness of the tunnel made no difference to the eyes of the spider. As the tunnel went deeper and deeper into the earth the smell of sulfur became ever more present. Soon the tunnel widened into a larger chamber that had two levels. The ceiling was jagged with pointed stalactites of every size that seemed to glow with an eerie phosphoresces. Some looked like columns of well sculpted pillars supporting the ceiling as stalagmites met stalactites. The second level was a snake-like riverbed that was ten feet deep with a jagged bottom of sulfur deposits, which ran through the center of the chamber. Bob maneuvered the spider through the pillars of stalactites and peered down into the bottom of the second level. Securing the end of a web to the edge of the drop off he lowered himself slowly down to the sulfuric bottom. He then laid down a perfect blanket of sticky web on the bottom of the riverbed, stretching from one side of the river to the next in a big square. He then grabbed two ends of the square. Reared up on his hind legs, picking up the sticky web blanket, he flipped it over onto the other side. The bottom side, now up, glowed from the yellow sulfur, which stuck to the web. Then using his two front legs he began to roll the sulfur coated blanket up. Using the spider's web, he secured the roll of sulfur to the spiders back like a giant spider backpack. Using the spider web, he had used to lower himself down, he climbed out of the riverbed. Making his way back through the pillars of stalactites he began guiding the spider back to them.

Finally, the spider arrived. Dameron and Modnar both took notice as the sound of the spider's foot falls could be heard coming up through the tunnel. As before the hideous head appeared before the body and they both shivered and ducked as the spider stopped just above them. A hissing sound could be heard and smoke appeared and went down the tunnel as the spider began to dissolve the remaining parts of the spider wall making the front end of the tunnel accessible again. The spider moved on and down the tunnel, to the place where the bones of the dead laid scattered around an old fire pit. The spider dropped the roll of sulfur next to the bag of potassium nitrate and began drooling spider saliva all over it, which left only a pile of sulfur, and made its way back to Bob. Once again the foot falls of the spider could be heard as it approached Bob and the others. The spider passed over them and stopped a few feet away from them. Bob flew over and landed on top of the spider and began to untie the stone from around the spider. Both Modnar and Dameron took to the air and flew down the tunnel. After untying the line around the spider's neck and removing the stone from about the spider's neck, Bob took to the air not knowing what to expect. The spider did not move. Bob flew over the spider and landed a safe distance in front of the spider. The four spider eyes each looked directly at Bob. The mist from beyond the spider and down the tunnel began to emerge once again and Bob could hear the clicking of the tiny creatures from within. Bob began to think of a speedy retreat. However, he noticed that the mist did not go beyond the giant spider. The spider seemed to be looking at Bob as if it were studying him. Bob began to wonder if it was possible that the spider shared his thoughts and had somehow bonded under the influence of the stone. The spider, after gazing at Bob for what seemed like a very long time, spun around and departed back down the tunnel from which it came, followed by the mist of little ones behind it. Bob then took to the air and went back to the camp sight.

The occupants of the camp site lived for many years before they met their demise. The fire pit that they had made was a hole in the ground they had dug and surrounded with stones. The charcoal of the items that had burned in the pit remained and there was such an amount that it was piled high above the stones. They knew what had to come next so they began milling the sulfur and charcoal at a ten percent and seventy-five percent ratio. This took only a few hours, but after that they added the potassium nitrate and began milling very carefully for four moons.

CHAPTER ONE
MEN OF MOUNTAINS

Trapped within the world, it's all they know. Foul and fevering, the sulfur burns within mountains of ice and snow. They built their halls and dwellings within the solid rock. The gold veins within the mountains enchanted them, the silver enticed them, and the sparkle of the diamonds found danced in their eyes. They forged the precious metals for centuries using the heat from the first volcano they encountered. They lined their special halls with it and studded it with diamonds. Geode tables filled the halls where they gulped their mead. They were once men that called the mountains their home. Now they were people from within the mountain. They channeled the heat from lava pools deep in the mountains that were yet to be volcanoes. They dug vents to channel heat and sulfur fumes from out of the mountains. They used lakes and melted glacier ice on the top of the mountains to cool their furnaces. Being once Mountain Men they knew how to trap and hunt. The only time they left the center of the mountains was to hunt for food or to bring in ice to preserve it. They devoted all their time to expanding their great empire deep in the mountains. Their presence grew more and more, with no one to stand in their way. Soon one mountain was not enough. They would dig tunnels from one mountain to the next so they would not have to venture outside into the freezing cold. When one mountain would become too crowded they would send out mining expeditions to discover new pockets of precious metals. They would be backed with warriors that would defend them and watch over the mining parties while they slept. Like settlers they would colonize each new mountain setting up new cities within them and enforcing their own laws. The first mountain is called Novarupta Katmai and was the largest of them all. Being the first one as well, it was the most populated and wisely protected by some of the most seasoned warriors they had. The first ones to start the mining and the creators of the first and most grand hall became rulers and governed all the mountains bringing them all together. Being the first to start the mining and discover the precious metals they were the ones who found a brilliant stone. The stones beauty shone unlike any stone ever seen. It was as if it possessed its own power and glowed from within. They decided to share this find and divide the stone into six equal parts. The six members of the council were Banden, Barrat, Flagen, Barpet, Domage, and Juhle. They were a council of men and with each and every new mountain city built, an ambassador would be nominated by them to be a representative of each one. The Mountain Mageik was represented by Tobine, the Mountain Martin was represented by Unckle, the Mountain Trident was represented by Rockten, the Mountain Griggs was represented by Monglen, and the Mountain Alagogshak was represented by Shotgen.

The Council soon discovered why the stone was truly significant by the greed of those who would try and steal the stones, but never survived long enough to enjoy them. For the stones would always open the mind's eye of the owner who would take control of the one who was in possession of the stone and destroy them. Growing tired of the constant killing they devised a plan on how this could benefit them as well as their society. Deep within the mountain they gathered together. They forged both steel and gold. A thin strip of gold was first forged by each one. Their stone was set within the gold. The ancient form of annealing was used to forge black steel that would fold over the gold that held the stone. So thin was the steel that they could fold it over a hundred times. They used crushed diamonds from the mines to line the edges within the steel and crushed diamonds were used again to sharpen the swords. The hilt of the sword was made of led surrounded by the black steel. A double edge was added to the swords and the words *JUDGMENT* was etched just above the hilt of every sword. Now the completed swords were all black without polish and very heavy so that no other person would ever consider wielding them. The Council took the swords and practiced many years with them. Combining strength and martial arts they soon found that they could kill a man and beast with one blow. Due to the weight, however, they would be lucky to land three blows and primarily would use the sword to block. Their plan, however, would never allow them to use the swords unless absolutely necessary. Since the stones were in the swords, whoever held the sword would be at the command of the owner. Therefore, if needed, someone would be elected to wield the sword for them. To test this and practice it they would solicit for volunteers who they would pay greatly if they survived or to their families if they did not. If they did survive, they would be in permanent bondage to whoever had chosen them. In one room they would put a beast with the volunteer and in a separate room they would hide. The sword would be given to the volunteer and the dance would begin. The councilman would look like a choreographer's dream as he took over the volunteer's body and slaughtered many a beast without even being there.

There were those of the mountain that the precious metals did not enchant and who decided to live outside the mountains. Some chose to live in the first of the tunnels, which were abandoned and used only for traffic. This was proven very hazardous though, due to the fact that there was no protection of the Council and there were many creatures that lived in the tunnels as well. Many died in their camps as they slept but there were some who survived and grew strong. Some went astray and developed their own ways and beliefs that were looked down upon by the Council. These people were banned from ever returning to the mountain cities. Two such people were Aguta and Ahnah.

OF AGUTA AND AHNAH

Aguta was brother to Ahnah and Dambar. Aguta and Ahnah were older than many of the people that were of the mountains—since before the thought of inhabiting within the mountains core was ever conceived. They were once advisors for the rulers. With Ahnah's abilities to communicate with unseen forces and Aguta's abilities to communicate with the dead they soon became very powerful. It was with this power that they began to conspire against the rulers and, without Dambar's knowledge, they used this power to place Dambar in the trust of the Council. They were going to use Dambar once he was a wielder of one of the swords. It was when Dambar was in possession of Tobine's sword that Ahnah tried to persuade a spirit entity to intervene and it was then that Tobine saw them for what they were. He communicated this to the rulers and they took action. Ahnah and Aguta were then banned from ever returning to the inner cities.

They dwelled mainly in caves within Mount Katolinat and Novarupta. It was in one of the caves of Mount Katolinat that they were fiercely attacked by Darkness. As they huddled around a fire they had built in the cave it came. The smell of sulfur became apparent as the light from their fire left the cave, chased out by the Darkness that would consume it. The flames of the fire no longer danced in the bright colors of yellow and orange. Instead, the flames slowly contorted in a dark purple and violet. As their eyes adjusted to the loss of light they began to notice dark forms on the walls and floor. It looked as if they were slowly searching for something like snakes slithering in human form. They were neither afraid nor secure in their thoughts of what was going on. They were familiar with practicing beliefs that often seemed of this nature. Ahnah was well versed in many levels or tiers of incantation meditations. They watched as it made its way toward them. Ahnah began to go into a meditation to free her mind from her body and search out what spiritual source may be behind this.

She sat on the floor knees together with her legs bent out along her sides. Her hands grabbed her knees her jaw dropped open. Her eyes remained open as her eyeballs seemed to roll back to look at her inward self. It was not long before dark figures reached Aguta. It started at his feet and began to form its way to the contour of his skin. Slowly it made its way up his body covering every inch of his skin.

Ahnah's spirit began at the very first level of the spiritual realm. Advancing quickly, she climbed her way up the many tiers of spiritual complexity and existence. She searched each level but found nothing in the area. Ahnah, having no sense of time in the spiritual world, did not know how long it had been before she found a level of consciousness that was in this vicinity. "What are you?" she asked it.

"Some call me Asmodeus, Mammon, or Asmodai," was its transmitted reply.

"What are you?" she questioned.

"When you can no longer bear yourself and cease to function that is me. When you become a slave to your desires that is me. When you want what others have that is me. When blood is spilt that is me. All those and more," it responded.

"What do you want?" she asked.

"I come for the souls of those who do not fear the Last Four Things."

The Darkness soon had covered all of Aguta's body and began to enter him through the nose like black smoke. "No please do not harm us," pleaded Ahnah.

"Why not? It seems that you are of this world and worship it greatly, so you are mine."

"We can help you," stated Ahnah.

"Ha," laughed the spirit. "How could you help me?"

"We can bring you bodies still alive with souls for you to take," replied Ahnah. It was at that instant her spirit was caught up into a tier of spiritual existence that she had never been to before. The Darkness, now in possession of Aguta's soul, brought him as well.

"Do you agree to this as well Aguta?" asked the spirit.

"Yes," replied Aguta. "If you release us we will do as we say."

"Very well then. I will release you till the time of your demise. You will grow old until the time that you bring me a soul at which point I will restore your youth or whatever ails you until you bring me another. Wherever the center of the world comes forth is where you can find me. Deliver them there." With that they found themselves back in the cave in front of the fire, unharmed.

CHAPTER TWO

Winter was fast approaching and deep in the mountain Novarupta, the rulers of the mountain empires were, Banden, Barrat, Flagen, Barpet, Domage, and Juhle. They sat in their great hall. Their chairs were carved from giant petrified redwood trees. The arm rests and seats were made comfortable with fur of the giant Kodiak bear. Their faces were white and smooth from lack of sun. Their long red beards were made short by braiding. They were old but strong, their steady diet kept them this way. Domage was the first to speak. "It is almost winter my friends."

"Yes," replied Flagen. "We must prepare ourselves for winter."

"Who will be willing to clear the outer caves for travel so that we may make the final hunt for the season?"

"I will," stated Barrat.

Banden began laughing, "It is my turn Barrat. You get to do it every year."

Juhle then spoke up, "I nominate Banden. He does a good job at that."

"I agree," said Barpet.

"Very well then, do we all agree that Banden clears the caves?" asked Domage. The great hall echoed with "aye."

Barpet then spoke up, "Who will wield your sword Banden?"

"You all know I would rather do it myself. But in order for me to make you all look good I will get Dambar to wield my sword." The hall erupted in laughter.

"Very well, good choice Banden," said Flagen. With that a messenger was sent forth to collect Dambar.

Dambar was a well-seasoned warrior who grumbled about everything and made up for the lack of hair on his head with the long braided hair on his face. He kept to himself mostly and people say that he seldom bathed just to keep people away. In Dambar's mind the only reason he would even consider doing this was due to the great reward that would follow its completion. In reality he knew he was bonded. Dambar was one the of rulers' favorite choices. He was single with no family and loved overwhelming odds.

Being very popular with the rulers meant that the messengers usually had no problem finding him, due to the fact that they were always being sent to get him. He usually could be found in any of the local taverns or brothels. When the messengers found him he was performing his morning ritual of praying to the community chamber pot. "Dambar, are you okay?" asked the messengers.

"Yes," he said. "I am just cleansing my soul from bad spirits. What is it you want?"

"You are needed at the great hall," said the messenger. "Very well, I will go," he replied. "But first I think I need a small nap," he said as he fell forward into the chamber pot. The messengers rushed toward him and started to pull him up. His once white beard was now glowing a mysterious green-yellow. As the messengers lifted him up, a goo oozed out his nose. He began to cough and sniff up the remaining goo into his flared nostrils. He rubbed his arms and hands all over his face trying to get the stuff off his face. He began to cough and the messengers asked if he was going to be okay. "Of course I am," he replied in his rumbling voice. He began blowing out his nose, which disgusted the messengers.

"Will you be able to meet with the rulers?" asked the messenger.

"Of course I will," he rumbled. "Tell them I will be there as soon as I get cleaned up.

"Very well," replied the messengers as they left him.

He stumbled over to the door of the room he was in and through it open. He swaggered through the doorway and into a larger room. There were many tables of wood and stone. No grand tables of marble and gold. The walls of this place had no diamonds or brilliant ore, only rough cave walls. There were a few patrons left asleep on the tables and some on the floor. A small table had four men there playing a mysterious game of stone cubes and two half-dressed women laughing. He looked around and found a small waterfall coming from an underground river high above the wall. It fell into a large pool of water contained by layered bricks of clay in a half circle. He flung himself, clothes and all, into the pool of almost freezing water. The four men with the women took notice and studied him for a while. He laid in the pool face down for almost thirty seconds before he popped up screaming. They laughed and returned to their game. This was not the first time that he had done something like this and it wouldn't be the last. The locals knew him for what he was and accepted him for who he was. They kind of looked after him with concern but kept their distance due partly to the fact that he spent most of his time and money there keeping the economy in this region going.

He lifted himself up and out of the water and onto the floor. There was a small opening in the center at the bottom of the bricks just opposite the waterfall. It drained into a gutter that flowed openly through the center of the room and into the kitchen quarters. He stepped out and looked down between his feet at the gutter. The water flowed clear for a moment before turning a glowing yellowish green for about four feet and then back to clear, leaving a long streak of green fluid between two columns of water. He followed it with his eyes as it traveled the length of the room. He grumbled a low, "Hmmm," to himself as it disappeared into the kitchen area. Screams of astonishment could be heard from within the kitchen. He laughed a low grumbled puff of a laugh and wobbled in the direction of the exit. He leaned forward to gain momentum and began his approach. When he came to the doorway he paused for a moment remembering what he was going out for. He then opened the door and stepped out into the busy hall. A rush of noise from hundreds of merchants and patrons talking loudly filled the air. The great hallway was lit by only a few torches mounted to the walls, but was then amplified greatly by the gold and translucent stones incrested within the walls. The stones were mostly green and blue in this hall and as the flames of the torches danced so did the tunnel dance of blue and green.

This hall was at the far side of the first district of the mountain. There were entrance tunnels at the base of the mountain. At the top of the mountain were old lava tunnels, which led to the open dome at the top of the mountain, which was blown open by the volcano many years ago. The cool air brought in at the base of the mountain was used to cool their hot forging furnaces and then blown up and out. The hot air would flow through a passage of tunnels cooling slightly before traveling through all the tunnels, up and out through the top of the mountain. When the furnaces were running, the air pressure generated would produce a five to ten mile an hour wind through the tunnels. So, when he walked out into the main hall the wind blew on the right side of his face. He stepped out into the hall and faced the direction of the wind. It felt warm and refreshing. He stood there for a while until the wind had dried his beard and it waved in the wind. He turned and looked at the hall and then at the door from which he had emerged. He always made sure to observe his surroundings before taking on one of the missions presented to him by the rulers. He knew that it might be the last thing he would remember before he dies.

Turning to the left he began his walk to the ruler's hall. The hallway was crowded with people. The people seemed to pay him no mind but kept a safe distance. He did not have to walk around anyone because the people would clear a path, not wanting to come in contact with him. He was used to this and liked what he thought was respect. Sometimes he did not even have to pay attention to where he was going, just as long as he was going in the right direction. This would leave him to his thoughts and the mental preparation of what he would soon be tasked to do. At the end of the hall of merchants it was less crowded and only a few stores for the rich remained. They were at the beginning and end of the hall of merchants for the convenience of the elders and rich, which were pretty much the same unless you were born into it. The hall narrowed and there was a ladder that began in the very center of the hall and went up at a seventy-degree angle to the top of a giant vat. There was a young lady at the top of the ladder. She was dressed in a flowing dark red dirndl with a white apron that went over her shoulders, around her neck, and tied in the back. She had shiny black hair that was cut in a Dutch fashion and was partly covered by a small white bonnet. She was slowly emptying her urn into the giant vat. He was lost in his thoughts and did not see the ladder. His heavy stature and momentum prevented him from stopping in time and he looked up as soon as he collided with the ladder and saw the woman falling. He did not, however, see the urn and as he put his arms out to catch the woman the urn and its contents fell on his head. His eyes burned as he held the young lady in his arms. She was light to him and was nothing to hold on to. He let her down and she could hear muffled curses coming from within the urn. She began calling him all kinds of names and informed him that he was going to have to pay for what he had just wasted. He reached up and pulled the urn from off his head and the rest of the contents left in the urn fell all over his face and over his clothes. When she saw his face she recognized him, and when he saw her, his face grew red with rage. The woman covered her mouth with the palm of her hand and began laughing hysterically. She apologized and told him that he did not owe her anything. Secretly she had wanted to do this for some time and new that most of the people in this mountain felt the same way. He wiped his burning eyes and blew a mist of the liquid out of his mouth. He looked at her blurred image through his burning eyes roared a loud roar that would have left most lions cowering. She disappeared quickly while he could not follow.

Now, not only infuriated with the fact he smelt like jasmine and lilies, he now had a bad taste in his mouth. There was nothing he could do. He had no time to change things. The rulers were waiting for him and he was on his way. Looking down the hallway he shook a shake that started with his head and went down his body to his toes, like a soaking wet shaggy dog trying to rid its soaking wet fur of water. He began walking further down the hall, leaving the shops and businesses behind. The brilliant lights began to fade and it almost became dark before entering the next section of occupied hallways. The brilliant hallway gave way to a more spacious plain looking area, which was one of the housing districts. The walls made of pure stone had stairways etched out of them. They zigzagged their way up the wall on each side for hundreds of feet with forty to fifty homes dug out of the rock on each landing. In the center was a large building for local gatherings and functions. Dambar kept his head down and tried not to make any eye contact with anyone. He quickened his pace with eyes focused on the ground. He could hear children playing and people talking. But that gave way to almost total silence to the ones who knew him and were trying to figure out why he was sporting this new scent. Finally, he was at the great hall leading to the rulers' meeting area. Its walls stood at least a hundred feet high. On each side stood a row of giant warriors carved out of black stone. Each warrior had torches for their eyes, which lit up the great hall with their gaze. Each warrior had a shield made of gold, which reflected the burning flame in their eyes. There was no other person or thing in this entryway leading to the rulers. The wind that blew through this hall made a low, hollow, echoing sound that made Dambar feel as if he was not alone, but with someone who understood how he felt. This hall had held thousands of warriors before, all coming to listen to the rulers to speak before going into battle. Their presence with their clinking armor and low voices seemed to absorb the sound of the tunnel even after they stopped to listen to the speech. But for now, it was just Dambar and with every step he took memories of great battles and days of glory would fill his thoughts. Now it was just him. Sometimes there would be large hunting parties, but with all the mountains occupied and too few people to colonize anymore, it would be some time before there would be battles to fight.

He finally came upon the great doors leading into the chambers of the rulers. The doors were a hundred feet tall and made with giant redwood trees hundreds of years old. They were held together by twelve-inch-thick steel cable within hemp lines. Each door had a handle made of brass that sparkled like gold. They were attached to the center of the door closest to the opening by a large steel chain. As Dambar approached the door, it was opened from the inside. It took several men pulling on the door handle to open it. The doors were opened both at the same time. A soft yellow glow creeped through the opening doors and filled the hall of the giant warriors causing their eyes to go dim in comparison. The smell of roast boar, freshly baked bread, and hot wine filled the air. There was a great table set before the rulers and as Dambar approached he knew that it was set for him. It was set so that he may have a great meal with them, before he would set out on his journey. It was very quiet in the chamber and his foot falls echoed within it. The rulers looked at him as he made his approach. He stopped just before the table next to a great chair just like the one the rulers sat on. The rulers looked at each other with a smile. They then turned their gaze upon him. Rockten began a slow giggle. Then another one began a low laugh. They looked at each other again before bursting out into loud bursts of laughter, slapping the arms of their chairs. Dambar was beginning to take offense and was about to leave when the faint smell of the perfume he was doused in caught up with him. His stern facial expression enhanced with the braiding of his beard and mustache was broken. His bottom lip blossomed out, the downward curve of his mustache curved up and he began to laugh also. They were all laughing greatly. Then as suddenly as they started they began to stop. Soon Dambar was the only one left laughing with his blackened teeth on full display. He soon realized what was going on and stopped laughing also. The room was once again silent. Dambar could not stop his stomach from protesting about the fact that there was all this lovely food and he had not eaten today. It echoed in the chamber. "Dambar!" stated Rockten with a small chuckle. "It seems to me that your stomach does protest too much."

"I think it's seeking retribution for the way it now smells," stated Monglen. "Sit down and eat Dambar and we will discuss what has come before us and what we need you to do." Dambar showed great enthusiasm and grabbed the arm of the chair with his right hand and jumped into the chair. He grabbed a rack of ribs from the roast boar and began to devour it in great earnest. The rulers began to laugh again as they too reached for some food. The great feast began and went on for at least a half an hour before Dambar stopped to gulp down a glass of warm wine.

"Dambar," stated Shotgen. "Are you ready for another mission?"

"Aye," said Dambar lifting his eyes from the meat to gaze upon the rulers. "It has been a long time since you have called on me."

"We would like you to clear out the abandoned caves at the foot of this mountain."

"It is hunting season and we need to send hunters out for one more hunt before winter arrives."

"It should be easy," replied Dambar. "This won't be the first time the caves have been cleared this year."

"True," said Shotgen, "but we have word that the spiders are back."

"What, those little things? I will take care of them no problem."

"There have been a few deaths in result of having them there. We have sent out hunting parties a month ago and they have not returned. We would like to hear the news that they are alive or dead."

"Very well sir, I will do it," said Dambar. Dambar rose from his seat, took a long swig of his wine and slammed it on the table. He thanked the rulers respectfully with a bow and left the chambers. Dambar faced the great door leading out. Two great men were on either side of him pulling on the door chain. As the doors swung open he could see a heavy black sword, which was now his to wield. It was held by an armored guard whose arms and legs were quivering by the weight of the sword. He walked over, took the sword and fastened it to his belt. A slight sigh came from the guard. Dambar looked at him and laughed.

Dambar began his journey through the maze of the mountain city all the way down to the opening that led him to the crude entrance tunnels. The smell of the damp cool air of the outside was familiar to him. He had been through here many times before. He knew most of it by memory although he knew things change down here. He left what was left of the light coming from the mountain city until he could not see his surroundings from the darkness. He sat down on the ground and waited an hour till his eyes could be accustomed to the darkness. Soon he could make out a dim light coming from the direction of the city so he walked even further until it was darker still. And then he sat for another half an hour until he could see his surroundings but none of the light from the city. He could not totally see his way around but could make out paths and used phosphorus, commonly found in rocks, in both red and white colors to navigate safely through the caves.

In a large room with only one chair made of a light wood sat Tobine. He meditated in a state of high awareness of his surroundings while conserving his energy. He knew at any moment Dambar may draw his sword and he would be required to take control of the fight.

Dambar navigated the cave at a slow pace keeping as quiet as possible. He did not want to be surprised in any way by some cave creature or creatures venturing through. Dambar began to think of all the creatures that he had encountered before. Different creatures came at different times of the year. Some go into the cave to sleep the winter away. Some came to sleep the summer away. Some just like to live in dark damp areas all together. There have been outcasts and deviants of his own kind living in these outskirts. Some he had become friends with and others were sworn enemies. An echoing sound could be heard coming from far down the cave. He could not make out what it might be. It was sort of a high pitch. It could have been some dripping water or some kind of crystal breaking and falling.

He sat for a moment and tried to determine which direction it might have come from. It was impossible to tell though. Sound travels a long way in these caves. Dambar stood up and continued down the cave. He came upon the midway point of the cave. When the caves were first being formed the rulers came upon a strange creature that killed many of the pioneers. The rulers had killed them all, they said, but they couldn't be sure. They were so impressed with them that they built statues of them on top of granite perches to ward off all predators that might enter the cave. This area of the cave had smooth floors and a spacious area for setting a camp and was used as a base camp while they mined the rest of the cave. This was the area that he once thought he saw one of the beings that were like the statue, but it was much smaller and could speak to him. It told him he was hiding from the light and the heat of the summer. It offered to help him hunt in the cave in exchange that he let him stay and never tell anyone. He accepted and after the season was over they were friends. Dambar thought this was a good place to rest for a bit. So he sat and pulled out some meat that he had acquired from the feast table before he had left. He inspected it, brushed off a few hairs that came from his clothing and ate it. He looked around a bit and then down the tunnel where he had to go. He then heard the sound that he had heard before, only it was close. He turned to face the direction from which the sound came. He then saw a piece of stone fall from one of the statues just below where its feet were perched. His hand went immediately to his sword. It rested there as his eyes squinted and focused hard on the statue.

Tobine was deep in meditation as he sat in his chair. He could hear the slight breeze that flowed through the room but he could not feel it. His mind was clear and well-focused when the window appeared in his mind. He was then in the cave. His hand rested on the sword handle. He saw the statues and knew where he was. There was something different and he wondered why he was so focused on one of the statues. His jaw dropped open as he took a breath of astonishment. He saw the statue breathing ever so slightly. It looked like it was sleeping. Its hairy ape-like body was only four feet tall. Its black leather-like wings were folded down on its back. Its mouth was closed and its canine razor-like teeth protruded out its mouth. The area around its mouth, nose, and eyes was hairless with the black leather-like skin of its wings. Tobine's mind started to flash with the screams of the pioneers, the bloody mess that followed and how the battle ensued. There was no mercy and they fought over their victims as they tried to steal them from one another. It was carnage of the worst kind. It was a feeding frenzy for the hungry.

It was a slippery slime sign of the time, its eyes open to unveil the cold green mind of an unseemly being. Slain ghosts from the past haunted his mind. No thoughts moved his body. He left his body and in the room of silence, he watched himself dance to the visions in his head. The horror from within the past of the cave guided his marionette commands. The demon's nostrils flared as if it got a whiff of something foul. Its eyes opened and Dambar drew the sword of Tobine. Dambar sniffed himself and cursed the perfume.

His arms, with sword in his left hand, swirled around each other in a liquid dance-like motion. He slowly approached the demon trying to force it into making the first move. Its wings folded back and its eyes blinked on and off simultaneously like little green lights. Its mouth opened and spewed forth a warning. Dambar slowly moved forward getting ever closer. The thing vomited up its last meal of a half-digested wolf. Its wings flapped and it took to the air. Though Dambar was being controlled by Tobine, his mind took note of the half-digested wolf rotting on the ground. He wondered if he rolled in it, would it be better than smelling like a woman. Dambar looked up as the beast defecated on him. It quickly flew around and came down on the back of Dambar. It bit into his thick fur coat and began to fly backward. It pulled him off his feet. It dropped him on the cave floor and flew back up again. It began to descend straight down on him. He lifted up his sword just as the creature was almost on him. He thrust it up only to have it grabbed by the hand-like feet of the demon. A tug of war ensued for a few moments until Dambar developed a rhythm and as soon as it was on the uptake he pulled down with all his might. He ripped the sword out of the grasp of the beast, slicing its feet and cutting off a few of its finger-like toes. It screamed loudly as it began to fly toward the cave entrance. Dambar, with sword in hand, started chasing it down the tunnel. He could not keep up with it though, but noticed as he began to slow down that it did not follow the exit. Rather it turned and went down one of the other tunnels that would lead to the old lava beds, up, and out of the volcano. When Dambar came to a stop he took a couple of deep breaths before he sheathed the sword.

Tobine awoke from his meditated induced trance. He could not believe what he had seen. If there was one of those things, there had to be more. Dambar was lucky the thing was not hungry. It would have been much worse if its stomach was empty when he encountered it.

Dambar let loose with a, "huummffff," and he sat on the cave floor. He had always thought it was a myth. Now that he had seen it, he had gained new respect for the old stories. He realized that he was very lucky and it may come back with more of them. He would keep his wits about him and if it did come back it would be an entirely different battle. He then heard a noise to the left of him. His thick eyebrow just above his left eye raised up as he looked over, drew his sword, and killed the furry tuff of an animal with a squeak. "Hmmmm," he said as if speaking to the dead animal. "I guess everything in this cave is going to seem a little mundane now that I have seen that thing." He stood up and stuffed the dead animal in one of the upper pockets of his coat. "Okay, let's get a move on," he said to himself. He began again slowly, stealthily, combing the caves of the area.

A few hours went by. He only encountered a few rats and a couple of large spiders but nothing really challenging. Dambar continued down the cave. He began searching all the different adjoining caves that led to cul-de-sacs. There were lava vents leading up and out that he did not care to waste his time climbing. They were far too dangerous and if that winged beast was in there he would be an easy target.

Dambar continued to work his way through all the caves making his way toward the final exiting cave. It was a long tiring search. He soon came to a lava bed. The lava bed was almost perfectly round. It was more like a tube or a vein that once pumped the blood from the heart of the earth through it. It was fifty feet in diameter. It was lined with jagged rocks. The bottom three quarters of the vein was covered in sulfur. The other upper quarter was charred black. It was almost as if someone painted these colors on the tunnel. These tunnels are the ones that make hollowing out a mountain for habitation easier. With these large tunnels equipment and supplies can be easily moved through the mountain. Lava tunnels usually ran north, south, up and down, providing access to almost the whole mountain. The trick is to make sure the inhabitance is above the tunnels, not below, and always make sure the proper air vents are built so that when the lava starts to flow again it will bypass your inhabitance and make its way out without choking them to death with toxic fumes. This tunnel meant he was only a few miles from the exiting tunnel. He walked a ways down the lava bed before coming to a hole that led to another tunnel. He turned and began venturing down it. He chose to stop at this point for a short rest. He spotted a stalagmite that had broken clean off about three feet of the cave floor. It was one of the larger stalagmites and was about four feet in diameter. As he sat his mind grew heavy with thought. He stared off into space with a thousand-yard stair. Without really thinking about it he reached into an inner pouch of his coat and pulled out a small tripod made out of a very light alloy forged within the mountains, extended its legs and set it before him. At the top of the tripod where the legs met hung a small hook. He then reached into his breast pocket and pulled out the small furry creature he had killed earlier.

It began to get very stiff so he had to pull on its front and back legs to stretch it out a bit. He then placed it belly down on the cold hard cave floor. He got behind the carcass, placed his foot on its back legs and held the tail up with one hand. With his other hand he reached down to his ankle and unsheathed a sharp knife. He cut upward from under the tailbone area, and cut through the skin until the tail was almost off, keeping a strip attached from the body to the top of the tail. He held the tail up, took his knife underneath, pulling and cutting the tail up the back. He brought the tail and a strip up the back of the carcass toward the head. He then inserted the knife between the meat and the skin of the beasty at the top part of the diamond shape of raw meat. Avoiding the side tissue he cut a couple of inches forward, moving the knife from side to side and cutting again on the other side of the diamond or square corner of the meat. Laying his knife aside, he held the tail and piece of skin loosely, and pulled up on the back legs. When he did this, part of the back and stomach begin to show under the skin. Next he pulled the front legs off the skin and cut at the joint of the carcass feet. Grasping the bit of skin left on the belly between his knife and thumb he pulled up breaking the front legs free from the body. He then turned the beasty over. The skin was hanging on both ends. He removed the internal organs before cutting off the head and back feet. Once the organs and genitals were out, he made a deep cut between the back legs. He pulled the legs backward, breaking the pelvic area apart. He then removed the anal intestine. Putting his two fingers in the deep cut he made, he held it up so the body cavity remained open. He then cut from the belly to the rib cage with his knife and pulled out all the vital organs. He then cut off both back feet and the head. Finished with prepping his meal he placed it on the hook on the tripod. His mind still wandered back to the beast back in the cave. He then reached into his jacket and produced four large coal bricks, and then some dry quarter-inch twine. He coiled the twine in a loose bunch and sprinkled it with a bunch of the hair from his kill. He then placed the coals on top of that. He then produced some flint and a stone and started showering the animal hair and twine with sparks. The animal hair soon started to fizzle, which caught the line on fire and the coals soon began to burn.

Dambar's mind mainly stayed on the thoughts of the flying ape thing. He started to work over in thought how he could better prepare himself if he encountered another one. Or what if he encountered more than one or two for that matter? His thoughts started to turn to memories of the stories he had heard of the great battle that ensued with the rulers when they first encountered them. He looked down on the cooking meat and thought of eating it right away. He knew he had to wait a little while longer even though the dead flesh was starting to turn a little brown. It was starting to smell good, which took his mind off of things for a while.

Ahead of Dambar and around one of the cave bends at the end of a cul-de-sac was a sleeping mother spider with her children underneath her. They too were sleeping. The smell of the cooking flesh was starting to make its way down the tunnels and toward the opening of the cave, which was actually higher than the point at which he was at. One of the baby spiders began to catch wind of the smell. It started to remind it of how flesh smelled when it was covered in its acid. It began to stir from its sleep. It bumped into one of its brothers who then woke up and in turn bumped into another, which started a chain reaction that woke up all the little spiders. Their black and purple little bodies all moving around together looked like a blanket of blackish purple bubbles all moving around. They all were sniffing the air and finding the location of where the smell was coming from. They soon decided it was time to move. The blanket began its journey down toward the entrance of the cul-de-sac. The only thing that stood in front of them was a pile of bones, which were once cave dwellers wrapped in their mother's webs. The blanket soon divided. Some went through the pile of bones intertwining through empty skulls, through the eye sockets, down spines, and around hip bones searching for any flesh that might remain. The other half went over the top, only interested in what might lie ahead of them. They soon joined together again to form a hungry purple blanket. The young spiders knew not how to control the acid that flowed from their main bodies to their mouths. So every time they got over excited the acid would spew from their mouths and on to the ground causing a smoke to rise up as it ate away at the cave floor. Smoke raised up above them ever so slightly. It rose up and then was left behind like a magic purple carpet leaving behind a trail of sparkling magic dust that faded away after it was only a few feet away from the spiders. The faint sound of clicking could be heard coming from them but it was almost too soft to hear. When the carpet reached the intersection of the cul-de-sac and was in the connecting hall it stopped. It turned to the right and stopped. They all sniffed a sniff in unison and then the carpet turned to the left. They all sniffed a sniff again and sighed. They decided they were facing the right direction and so on they went, leaving an even thicker puff of magic dust.

Dambar had finished cooking his meal and now was taking dainty bites out of his well-cooked kill. The purple blanket descended down an almost blackened tunnel until it came to a small plateau that was level with Dambar's position. They were only a few hundred feet away but they had to descend even further down and climb back a steep incline before they could reach Dambar. Dambar thought he heard snapping sounds so he looked down at his fire thinking that he had put it out. Recognizing that it was in fact out he listened again. He turned his head hard to the right and looked at the plateau that was across from him just as the purple blanket descended down the cave and out of sight. Dambar returned to his meal.

He became entranced again with the earlier thoughts of the flying creature. He assumed the position of the thousand-mile stare as the purple blanket rose up behind him on the cave floor.

The mother awoke softly from her sleep. Her top left eye slowly opened and then her lower right eye opened. Her lower right eye looked down underneath her and then it looked straight ahead for a second before all eyes were open. She stood straight up on all legs and looked underneath her. Acid quickly flowed to her mouth and dripped on the cave floor leaving small potholes in the cave floor. She quickly spun around and charged down the cul-de-sac. When she came to the intersection of the cul-de-sac and the main tunnel she turned to the right and listened. She waited to see if her children were about. Not seeing or hearing them she turned to the left and listened and waited. She sniffed the air and realized that there was a slight smell of burning flesh in the air. It was mingled with the smell of burning fur. She was pleased with the thought that her little ones had finally grown up and made a kill of their own. She could hear a sound though. It was a low steady tone. It was a ways off and coming up from down the cave. She could also hear the clacking sound of her children's feet. Dambar came running up from the depths of the cave, his hair, back, legs, and arms were all smoking with the burning acid and a few of the small spiders were flapping in the air like a small kite holding on to strips of smoldering clothing. The purple blanket followed close behind. The mother backed up in surprise and shock. Her eyes focused hard on Dambar. She reared back and let loose with a giant burst of webbing. It opened up like a large ring of puffed smoke. As it flew through the air she fired off five or six smaller bursts that attached themselves from one side of the circle to the next. She formed a crisscross pattern within the circle much like a dream catcher. Dambar was looking behind him to check his progress as he came up from the tunnel. He turned around just in time to see the spider-spun net right in front of him. It folded around him and clung to him like a strong rope. It tripped up his feet and bound his arms to his side. He then fell face first on the floor, knocking him unconscious. When his body slid to a stop the mother quickly came up to the now unconscious Dambar. The children were not far behind and after plucking a few of the children that were clinging to Dambar off she walked over the top of him and started defending the catch from the greedy little children that were eager to tear Dambar apart. She picked Dambar up and put him on her back and walked back down the cul-de-sac. She climbed to the top of the pile of bones. She looked up and shot a short blast of web to the cave ceiling, which hung down to just about ten feet above the pile of bones. She then suspended Dambar upside down from the dangling line. She then walked further down the cul-de-sac turned and spun a few more feet of webbing around Dambar just to make sure he was secured. She called to her children and they came with some hesitation. They were no longer the happy smoking purple blanket they once were. She corralled her children at the end of the cul-de-sac and kept all four eyes on them for the rest of the night.

CHAPTER THREE

Bob, Dameron, and Modnar stood over their finished product. After all their labor they all had the feeling that it was only half of what they needed. Bob began to psych himself up for another round of processing the elements, but it would be tough going without the help of the spider. Their thoughts were soon interrupted by a sound coming from down the tunnels. It was a single solid note with a duration of almost a minute. It started out low and faint but grew louder. They all turned into the direction from which the sound was coming. It was almost as if they could see the sound. It came closer and closer until it passed them by and ventured passed them and became an echo up the tunnel. It finally left the mountain like a voice from the skeletal whale. "Interesting," was the statement from all of them at the same time in an almost mesmerizing tone. As if they were in a trance they began walking down the tunnel in an attempt to investigate the origin of the sound.

The clear tunnel soon gave way to a larger tunnel filled with stalactites and stalagmites of unusual size and shape. Some were crooked with one or more points. Kind of like a saguaro cactus. Some of them were almost a perfect cone shape in various sizes. The cave continued down in steep drops onto a plateau and then dropped again. Every time the plateau would give way to a steep drop they would casually open their wings and glide down to the next plateau. It came so natural, like breathing, that they did not even have to think about it. They were almost across the first plateau when the pouch that was tied around Bob's waist began to glow. Bob stopped and looked down at the bag. A bluish green glow was slowly pulsing from within the bag. Dameron and Modnar were on either side of Bob. "Rakkii na hito ne," said Dameron in a surprised tone of voice. Bob looked at him with a half sarcastic smile. Suddenly the bag rose up from Bob's waist and began to tug on Bob's waist. It was like someone had grabbed a hold of the bag and was pulling on it. Bob grabbed the bag and held fast to the stone that was inside. The force that was pulling on the stone became stronger and Bob began to fear that the stone would rip out of the bag. His grip on the stone became more intense and his wings spread out from his side. Dameron and Modnar stood aside and watched Bob slowly float down the tunnel. They were so amazed they just stood there in awe as Bob slowly disappeared down the tunnel.

Dambar began to awaken slowly. His eyes slowly opened but his vision was blurred slightly. He did not know where he was and he wondered why he was hanging upside down. His vision was coming back and the first thing that came into focus was a scull looking up at him. His body shivered and he let out a slight gasp. He looked around as the memory of what happened slowly came back to him. The web clung to his body. Half his face was covered in the sticky goo-like web. He soon found himself swinging back and forth slowly. He could see the giant spider at the end of the cul-de-sac. The little spiders and mother were all asleep. He tried his best to remain silent.

He looked up and noticed that the hilt of his sword was glowing and was trying to pull away from him. His swinging became more and more to one side than the other. Soon the swinging had stopped and he remained at a forty-five-degree angle. His eyes opened wide as the whole pile of bones came into view.

Modnar and Dameron began to chase after Bob. They too took flight to avoid all the stalagmites, stalactites, and some of the jagged cave flooring. They navigated their way through the tunnel close behind Bob. The obstacles in the cave were becoming very numerous. They soon had to divide the cave up into three flight patterns so they all could fit through. They were weaving in and out. Sometimes someone would get ahead of Bob and have to cut back. There were a few close calls with Modnar and Dameron as they would attempt to cut back and find themselves on a collision course. Finally, the cave narrowed and the obstacles gave way to a clear, more apparent path. They began to round a bend in the tunnel. They were putting a great distance between them and the opening of the cave. The once cool air that was keeping them at a comfortable temperature was no longer present. As their body temperature began to increase they began to feel lethargic and slow. Bob noticed that up ahead the cave was about to split. He had no idea which direction he was going to go. It seemed like he was headed directly for the connecting point of the cave wall. He started to anticipate which way he was going to go so he pointed himself down the direction of the right cave. He slowly started to bank and thought he had made the right choice. Suddenly though the bag tugged hard on him and pulled him down the left tunnel. Both Dameron and Modnar flew past Bob and down the right tunnel with surprised looks on their faces.

Bob saw the pile of bones down the tunnel and the web sack that dangled above them. The stones pulsating light was now a steady bright light. He noticed that there was a light within the web sack just like his stone. All kinds of thoughts started to go through his head. Bob noticed something within the web sack and it seemed that his stone was headed for the light that was within the web sack. Bob braced for impact and he collided with Dambar.

Both Bob and Dambar were now swinging above the pile of bones. Almost immediately a window opened up in Bob's mind. He could see Tobine and Tobine could see him. There was a great pause as they both were trying to absorb what was happening. Dambar squirmed for a short while but then gave up with a sigh the moment he caught on to what was happening. His eyes rolled back into his head as Bob went into conversation. "Who are you?" he said.

"Who am I? Who are you?" said Tobine. There was a slight pause and he spoke up again. "What is going on here?"

"Your guess is as good as mine," said Bob.

"Where is Dambar?" questioned Tobine.

"Hahahaha! Dambar is that you?" asked Bob.

"Yes," grumbled Dambar. "How do you know me and why can't I move my arms?"

"It seems that you have been captured by a giant spider," said Bob.

"Get Dambar loose this instant," demanded Tobine.

"I will leave that up to Dambar," said Bob. "Dambar would you like to be freed?"

"Yes," grumbled Dambar.

"Very well then," said Bob to Tobine, "I will free him." Bob drew Dambar's sword and sliced open the web sack. Dambar began to struggle. "Don't struggle," said Bob in a very monotoned voice, trying not to wake the spiders. It was too late though. Dambar was fueled by anger mixed with fright and just wanted out. Dameron and Modnar came up behind Bob just in time to see Dambar falling toward the pile of bones. They had seen the giant spider and its little ones. They knew they had to prevent him from falling on those bones, which would surely wake the spiders.

Dambar, falling headfirst toward the skeletal remains, put his hands out in front of him to break his fall. He closed his eyes in anticipation of impact just as Dameron came up and grabbed his hands. Modnar grabbed his feet and started flying him down the cave and away from the spiders. Bob remained with the sword and in communication with Tobine. "Do you hold the sword," asked Tobine.

"I do," said Bob.

"So why can't I control you?"

"Don't know. Why should you be able to control me just because I hold the sword?"

"There is a stone in the sword," said Tobine.

"Ah, I see," said Bob. "I understand now. I also have a stone and it led me to Dambar."

"Hmmm," Tobine pondered. "I think we should meet."

"I don't think so," stated Bob.

"Why not?" asked Tobine.

"We are of two different worlds," said Bob. "I would not be able to live in yours."

"Very well," said Tobine. "Could you give the sword back to Dambar?"

"I can do that," said Bob as he spread his wings and flew over to Dambar. Bob asked Dambar if he would like his sword back.

Dambar nodded his head and said, "Put it in the sheath so he cannot control me, I don't know what he will do." Bob sheathed the sword and the communication between Bob and Tobine ended.

Dambar sat on the ground. Bob, Dameron, and Modnar stood on the ground before him. "Many thanks my little friends," said Dambar. "I probably owe you my life."

"It's good to see you again my friend," said Bob. Both Modnar and Dameron looked at Bob.

"You mean you know this being?" asked Modnar. Dameron smacked Modnar on the shoulder. Modnar grabbed his shoulder.

"Show some respect," said Dameron.

"Dambar, would you mind if we headed toward the cave entrance? It is a tad warm here and we are not feeling so good," said Bob.

"Of course not, I forgot you were so sensitive to the heat. They began walking down the cave toward the entrance.

"Is that perfume I smell Dambar?" asked Bob.

"Yes," grumbled Dambar. "It's a long story."

They talked as they ventured toward the entrance. They came to the part of the tunnel that had different levels of plateaus and there were steep inclines. Dambar would spread his arms out and Modnar and Dameron would grab a hold of each arm and fly him up to the next plateau so he could continue his conversation with Bob. Dambar went on about his adventure with the spider and how he got surprised and overwhelmed by the purple carpet. "Those nasty little things," he said. "I have never seen them in such abundance." He went on to talk about his latest encounter with a nasty ape-like thing with wings. Dambar stopped short just after finishing and backed up a few steps so that Bob, Dameron, and Modnar were in front of him. He looked at them and asked, "Any relation?" They looked at each other and shrugged their shoulders. Modnar put one arm across his chest and cradled his chin in his other hand.

Looking down he said, "There is that one female, Famdon, that does have hair in quite the most—" His sentence was cut short by a hard slap in the middle of the back by Dameron.

"Heeeeyyyy!" shouted Modnar.

Dambar let loose with an interesting, "Huummmfff," kind of almost an observational laugh. They continued on down the tunnel. It was beginning to get cooler and Bob, Modnar, and Dameron began to feel more like themselves. They were now past the lower plateaus and were weaving around the stalagmites and stalactites. Bob began to start with his story and how he acquired the stone. He told about living in darkness, but now he had light within the darkness after hearing the words spoken to him that he understood. He spoke of how after hearing the words he knew he was not of this world and how we are all just visitors or transients in a proving ground of faith.

"There is a war out there," he said. "It's a battle between two worlds. That of which one is worldly and one that is not."

There was a long silence as they walked along. It was as if all of them were pondering and digesting the words Bob had spoken. It seemed like only a short while as time usually passes when deep in thought, but it had been almost an hour. They were crossing the final lava tunnel where Bob had used the spider to gather sulfur. Dambar was the first to speak. He told Bob that he now knew why the rulers were the way they were. He said he knew the secret of the swords and now he knew why they had such calmness to them, even when they were in harm's way and surrounded by stress. He admitted that he did not totally understand or believe all of it, but there was some truth to what Bob had spoken of.

They soon came to the camp that had the bones of the people that had died. They stood around the camp and Dambar surveyed the scene. He noticed that the ashes from the fire had been removed and the bones of the dead had been moved about. Dambar then noticed a large sack on the ground that smelled of black powder. Dambar turned toward Bob and asked him if he had done this. Bob nodded. "To what end?" asked Dambar.

"I cannot tell you everything yet," said Bob, "but what would you think of colonizing another mountain?" Dambar thought about it for a short while.

"I can't say. It would be foolish of me to answer, due to the fact that I could not do it alone and I would not want to offend the rulers of these mountains. What mountain did you have in mind?"

"It is past the Valley of Ten Thousand Smokes and next to the Falling Mountain," said Bob.

"You mean Mountain Cerberus?" replied Dambar.

"I do not know all the names of all the mountains but that may be the one," stated Bob. "How do you plan on making the mountain inhabitable? We came here to make enough black powder to maybe blast our way into the mountain. I don't think we have enough, however. If you could you speak to the rulers and if I could gain their support they may give us more black powder to work with."

"I still don't see what's in it for you," Dambar said. "But I will ask."Aguta and Ahnah

They were finishing up dinner. It was three pm and it had already started getting dark. The sun was down and casting a sky of pink behind the mountain range. They had spent the summer up in Novarupta after traveling to the Valley of Ten Thousand Smokes and the Knife River. They slept in the abandoned caves on the outskirts of mountains from which they had been exiled, hunting sheep and storing the dead flesh in the Knife Creek Glacier for future use.

Typically, the meat would freeze overnight in the glacier and stay that way. Now that winter was coming they moved down into the valley just below the Baked Mountain where there would be less wind and they could store there meat outside in a pit they had dug and covered with wood to prevent animals from getting at it. They had trained two wild wolves that they had come upon when they were pups. They killed their mother and ate her flesh and used her pelt for clothing. One was harnessed and pulled a small boat or canoe that they filled with their belongings and the other was harnessed to carry their teepee.

In the mountain Katmai, just beyond the mountain range that Aguta and Ahnah had stayed in, small amounts of smoke were escaping from out of the top and a few thousand feet above at the top was a hot spring that was kept warm by sulfur gasses from deep within the mountain. There was no snow on the top of this mountain nor around the hot spring, and during the winter the whole place stayed at about fifty degrees. Aguta and Ahnah were not interested in this place though because there would be no way to keep their food frozen. That is if they could find food there. They were happy in their frozen world, much like the colonies.

They were not in the valley to stay, however. They had plans to move farther west and south. They ventured to the lower half of the Valley of Ten Thousand Smokes. They then traveled through the valley between the volcanoes Majeik, Martin, and the Buttress Range. They went past Alagogshak and across the frozen Becharof Lake. Their destination was the Gas Rocks and the search for souls so corrupt that it would please their master.

Aguta and Ahnah approached the area of the Gas Rocks. The heat generated by the cluster kept the area in the sixties year-round. The

Gas Rocks cluster consists of three dacite domes and one stratified fragmental mafic cone. A second mafic cone exposed in a lakeshore bluff due west of the Gas Rocks. Viewed from a distance, the three high knobs that make up the Gas Rocks include two of the domes and the mafic cone was the southeastern-most knob. These Gas Rocks were vents that led to the center of the earth through many twisty tunnels that joined other tunnels. They were part of many vents around the world. Ruler of all that is material dwells in the center of the world gathering souls for its army that will be released by Worm Wood. Wisps of smoke escaped the vents like tongues of the beast searching out and licking at souls so corrupted by the world they could never leave.

Aguta and Ahnah began to set up camp. Saxifrage grew wild and in abundance in the area, which made a soft ground for them to pitch tent and lay in. Ahnah began to set up their teepee. He opened the cover out flat, with the right side up. He selected four of the strongest poles for the quad pod. One pole was laid on the cover, with the butt end next to the door, even with the bottom hem and the other end extending past the tie between the smoke flaps. The other two were laid on the cover, side by side, approximately one-third of the distance around the bottom of the cover. Once again the butt end was placed even with the hem and the other end extending past the tie at the top. He tied the four poles together at a point approximately fifteen inches above the point where the poles crossed each other. The poles were tied together firmly, but not extremely tight. When the quad pod was set up, the knot tightened but not so tight that the poles would break. The poles were tied with a rope long enough to reach the ground plus four or five extra feet, so that it could be staked down in the center of the teepee in the event of strong winds. The quad pod was then set up as he walked under the poles. He spread the quad pod apart so the ends were spread evenly in the approximate diameter of the teepee. Starting at the front, he staked the rest of the poles in the crotch at the top. He saved two of the longest poles for the smoke flaps and left one pole out directly opposite the door. He then took hold of the rope hanging down from the tripod poles and walked with it to the outside of the frame. He walked the rope around the circumference of the teepee poles three times to wrap all the poles together at the crotch. The remaining length of rope was then brought back inside the frame and staked to the ground at the center.

The cover was rolled up from both sides to the center, having the tie at the top exposed. He then slid a pole under the cover and tied the pole to the cover, using the tie at the top. The butt of the poles were now even with the bottom of the cover. Aguta held the butt end to the ground while Ahnah lifted the pole and cover into the open spot left at the back of the frame. He then unrolled the cover around the frame. Starting at the top, he put sticks in the holes that held the front of the cover together. The left side went over the right side. He staked the bottom out and adjusted the poles so the cover lay smooth. He put the ends of the two remaining poles in the pockets that were at the top corners of the smoke flaps. Ahnah stepped back to admire his work. He was very pleased with the artwork he had done on the outside. They had stained the outside with animal blood in the shape of the skulls of the animals they had killed to make it.

Aguta began to unpack the canoe. There was a spear, two ulus, some meat, a bag of black powder, furs for their bedding, two Yukłuktaak's made from bone, a Bola, and in the center of the canoe was a bag with several dormant Mongolian death worms. The ulus had handles that were made from human bones in which they had etched the likeness of the ones they had belonged to. The Mongolian death worms were Ahnah's favorite animal and she kept many of them in a bag full of sand. She picked up a few when they traveled Gobi. It is a sausage-like worm over three feet long, and thick as a man's arm, resembling the intestine of cattle. Its tail is short, as if it were cut off, but not tapered. It is difficult to tell its head from its tail because it has no visible eyes, nostrils, or mouth, but may have them on some occasions. Its color is dark red, like blood or salami. It can kill at a distance either by spraying an acid-like substance or by using an electrical discharge. The worm lives underground, hibernating most of the year except for when it becomes active in June and July.

Behind the canoe was a large bag that was tied to the end of the canoe with a three-foot-long rope. Within the bag was an unfortunate native of the region that they had encountered near the end of their travels. The Gas Rocks started to become active. A heavy white gas oozed out of the rocks. It spewed out and moved around inches off the ground. Aguta went over and untied the sack from the canoe. He began dragging it over close to the rocks. Ahnah walked over and grabbed the bag of Mongolian death worms. The activity of the Gas Rock had warmed the area up almost ninety degrees. The bag that held the worms was moving slowly. Aguta emptied the contents of the sack on to the ground as Ahnah dropped the open bag containing the worms next to the body. The worms oozed slowly out of the bag. They began to slink slowly around the body leaving behind a trail of goo. It was almost as if they were salivating slightly, trying to make the moment last as long as possible, savoring every second. Soon all the worms had encircled their victim. The unconscious body in the center started to come to. His eyes opened a little and focused on the worms just before all the worms let loose with an electronic pulse. His limp body arched as a scream echoed across the icy waters. Now paralyzed by the worms he could do nothing but watch the worms close in on him. Their once worm-like heads opened up to reveal a circular set of razor teeth. The only thing their victim could do was show the horror in his eyes. They began to feast on the flesh laid out before them. No blood ever touched the ground as the worms gorged themselves on everything. Their bodies became bloated and bright red with the flesh and blood. Acid oozed from their mouths, making the bones soft and chewable. It was now the time for the center of the earth to have its turn. By now the smoke had reached the body and was moving up the legs. His eyes moved down to witness the smoke covering his body. It finally reached his head and entered his body through his nose. His eyes widened as it filled his lungs and made its way through the body. Finally, his eyes seemed to fill up with the smoke like a glass bowl being filled with milk until all you could see was white. The smoke soon imprisoned his soul. As it left the body it was dragged down into the depths of the earth. The spiritual friction of a soul being torn from its state of being into a state of slavery produced a static charge. This positive static charge created a streamer that began reaching up toward the sky. At this time a stepped leader of negative charge, invisible to the eye, began descending from the clouds above. It began zigzagging its way downward in roughly fifty-yard segments and in a matter of milliseconds. The negatively charged stepped leader met the positive charge. A powerful electrical current began flowing. A return stroke of bright luminosity traveling sixty thousand miles per second shot back toward the cloud. A flash of white light was generated, reflecting blue through the moist atmosphere.

This light lit up the ground and caused the bottom of the clouds to light up in an eerie blue light. The lightning was answered back with the call of thunder that echoed through all the canyons in the area. The worms finished their feast and lethargically sloshed their way toward their sack, leaving behind a deflated soulless corpse.

Once the soul-filled smoke reached the center of the earth with its prize, a new thick mist arose from the depths of the earth. It was thick and heavy and oozed forth. It went toward Ahnah and Aguta. It began at their feet and swirled up their legs. When it reached the main body it rose up and covered the whole body. Whatever diseases infected them was cured and whatever aging had occurred was reversed. They were as they once were at the time of their first earthly ritual performed many years ago.

CERBERUS

As Bob, Modnar, and Dameron walked through the blowing snow, their bodies became one with the environment and their skin began to change. They began to grow larger. Their skin developed fish-like scales that were white as snow. The scales seemed to reflect the brightness generated by the snow. Their eyes turned a blue that only glaciers seemed to capture. Their finger and toenails began to turn purple. They disappeared in the snow drifts like winter ptarmigan.

In the depths below the sea of blowing snow and ice lingered the flight of razor sharp talons, life stealing beak, and fiery yellow eyes. The invisibility of the three souls reflecting light was stolen by the thief with yellow eyes. Its hunger for carnage that keeps it alive never ends. Its snowy white plumage rendered it as invisible as the souls themselves. The shrieking siren from above was almost as razor sharp as its talons themselves. The two dots of yellow descended upon the souls getting larger and larger as it descended upon them.

As Modnar, Dameron, and Bob walked on top of the snow the wind whipped past their ears in low whispers of delight. They were in their element and Bob led point. Dameron and Modnar were just behind him on either side. Their scales were hardened by the cold almost like a sort of armor protecting them from the elements. It was nighttime, but the bright snow almost had an eerie light of its own. They kept their gaze forward as they knew they were going in the right direction but were not really sure of what laid ahead of them. A giant almost prehistoric snow owl approached them from behind. They stopped as the faint shriek of the owl could barely be heard by them from the low howl of the wind. Bob turned around just in time to see the owl right behind them. Its talons were stretched forward ready to close around Dambar and Modnar. He froze partly from disbelief and shock at the huge yellow eyes. Both talons grabbed Dambar and Modnar before they could turn around. Bob looked up just in time to see the huge beak open and grab his head and shoulders. The owl flew into the blizzard sky with its prizes. Bob struggled to loosen himself from the beak. As he struggled, the owls tongue licked him in the face as if tasting him. A total feeling of disgust came over him. As his face was now dripping with slobber. Their protective scales were the only thing that protected them from the sharp beak and talons of the owl.

After the last ride Bob had them on, Modnar and Dameron were quite comfortable in the clutches of this eagle snow owl. It held them securely face down through the air. Bob, however, was totally uncomfortable. Both Modnar and Dameron took great pleasure in that fact as they grinned ear to ear during the whole ride. The storm was starting to subside. The winds began to die down and now the snow was falling slowly down in small swirls. They were high in the air. Bob from the waist down was a wiggly worm trying to free himself. His arms were pinned to his sides and he could not break free. He soon gave up and became a wet noodle in the bird's beak. He was finding it hard to breathe. He had to time his inhales with the bird's inhales just to get air. It was uncomfortably warm in the bird's beak. If the bird did not land soon he would lose his protective scales. The owl began to circle high in the air. It was above its nest and was spiraling down to it in a slow descent. The nest was high in a tree and large enough to hold two grown men. Modnar and Dameron looked down on the small black dot until it got larger and larger. They began to see two white dots in the center. One of the dots was larger than the other. As they got closer they recognized one of the white dots as a baby bird. As they got closer they began to hear the baby owl screeching, but they could not make out the other white circle. Soon the giant owl dived straight for the nest. It dived down below the nest and then came up again right in front of it. It ran out of momentum just above the nest and came down. Its feet came down on either side of the giant white dot in the center squishing both Modnar and Dameron. The mother's beak, filled with Bob, was crammed down the throat of the baby owl. The baby owl jerked its throat and swallowed Bob whole. The mother owl then released Modnar and Dameron for the consumption of the baby bird and flew off in search of another meal. Both Modnar and Dameron stood up. They then realized that the other larger dot was a pile of bones. They looked at the baby owl, which was screeching at the top of its lungs and looked like it was going for seconds and thirds. Knowing the bird was old enough to fly they both dove into the pile of bones to hide themselves. Bob could not believe that he was in the stomach of a baby owl. He took out the stone and placed it against the baby owl's stomach with the rope around his neck. The window opened in his mind and he could see through the owl's eyes. He saw the pile of bones in the center of the nest. He looked to the right and to the left but he did not see Modnar or Dameron. The pile of bones was quite high so he jumped over the pile of bones. There still was no sign of them. He spun around and looked again at the pile of bones. A few of the bones at the top of the pile began to move and then fall aside as Modnar's and Dameron's heads poked out of the pile. Bob could see the back of their heads. It was so very warm in the belly of the owl and Bob could not take it any longer. Bob began to induce vomiting just as Dameron and Modnar turned around looking for him and the owl. They turned around just in time to see the baby owl hacking like a cat trying to cough up a furball. With its wings spread out, it arched its back with its head down and began with a wheezy short cough. It started in very slow convulsions. *Hack...hack...hack...hack.* Then it became faster, *hack, hack, hack, hack,* and finally *bluuaaack.* Bob came spewing out in slow motion with other undigested bits of who knows what.

He came out first with the rope around his neck and when the stone finally reached the owl's mouth it held on to it keeping Bob in control. Bob hung from the owlet's mouth swinging ever so slightly with goo dripping of his body. His hands grabbed hold of the rope just above his neck. He lifted himself up and out of the loop. His hands held tight to the rope and the owlet began to swing him back and forth slowly. Higher and higher he swung until he was flung onto the back of the owlet. He then had the bird let go of the stone just long enough to bring it around the neck of the owlet and loop it around like a bridle. Dameron and Modnar looked at Bob with his hair so badly matted and squished he looked like some kind of gooey spider form. Bob gave them an evil grin which they had seen before. They knew exactly what was about to happen so they both charged the owlet sending bones flying off in all directions. They came around behind the bird and jumped on its back just behind Bob and held on as the owlet jumped out of the nest. It fell a few feet before the wings opened up slowing their descent. It glided a few feet before taking off into the sky.

The full moon was high above the mountains, lighting up their snow-covered peaks and leaving the valleys below dark. It was as if the mountain peaks were alive with their own power, glowing mysteriously and wondrously. Above the moon the sky was dark with many layers of clouds. As the owlet rose into the sky with its passengers the moon seemed to be following them. Soon the owlet disappeared into the clouds entering a world of freezing cold darkness. It was only a short while before they passed through the first layer of clouds. They then found themselves between two layers of clouds. Snow was falling from the layer of clouds above them to the layer below them. The moon had followed them up into the sky between the layers of clouds and its light shone brightly through the falling snow giving the feeling of life within a snow globe. The owlet stopped flapping its wings and began gliding. They looked toward the moon in awe before the layers of clouds merged together. It was as if the moon wanted one last look at them before it would disappear down behind the mountains. The owlet banked to the right and began its descent toward the earth.

As they fell below the layer of clouds, it was as if their presence was being announced to the earth below. The atmosphere flashed with a bright blue light and a roaring thunder struck them with its vibration. Sunrise was approaching and they were tired, hungry, and needed to find shelter soon. The lake below Mount Cerberus was coming into view. The owlet began a fast descent. Bob, Modnar, and Dameron leaned forward almost lying flat on the owlet's back. The owlet, only a few short feet off the ground, opened its wings and swooped up shortly losing momentum and dropped to the ground. It screeched a loud ear-piercing, high-pitched screech as Dameron and Modnar jumped off. Bob slowly removed the stone necklace from around the owlet. The owlet screeched again and Bob hopped off. The owlet hopped up and spun around to look at Modnar, Dameron, and Bob. It shook its head and fluffed its feathers until it looked like a giant fluff of feathers. Its head slowly spun around in a slow three hundred and sixty degrees, looking at them again and blinked its eyes. Bob had that feeling again that somehow they had shared something. The owl's head spun back around again and gave them a wink as it spread its wings and took off into the sky. The frozen lake below the mountain lay before them. The wind in the area had blown the lake free of snow and polished it to a glassy perfection. They walked over to the shoreline and looked toward the canyon to the left that was divided by two mountains leaving a very narrow passage. The pressure of winds swirling around on the other side of the passage was building up. They laid their hands on the frozen ice covering the lake. The roar of the wind that was being forced through the passage filled the air as they recharged themselves on the lake ice. White streaks scattered across the lake ice as they drew the power from it. Soon the ice turned a mossy green color as the wind broke free from the passage and swirled around them. They spread their wings and rose into the air and dipped back down as to not be blown away by the wind. When the gust of wind had stopped they dropped back down to the lake shoreline. A small pile of rocks lay just a short distance from them. The tundra had grown over it and it looked like it might have been once occupied by a family of foxes. They quickly flew over to the pile before the wind could come back in their direction. They reached the opening and entered it. It was a tight fit but they manage to squeeze in one at a time to find that the inside was much larger than they thought it would be. It might have been the den of an arctic fox or something larger. They brought in as much snow as they could to line the inside and to block the entrance so that whatever might come back would have to dig its way in, giving them full warning of its approach.

Modnar lay stretched out on the frozen floor of their temporary shelter. He awoke from a dream but kept his eyes closed. It felt so nice to just lay there in the icy warmth of winter. He then began to remember his dream. There was some sort of bubbling liquid involved. The thought of warm liquid made him appreciate the cold even more.

"It wasn't a dream," stated Bob. Modnar slowly opened one eye to see Bob sitting legs crossed across from him.

"What do you mean?" replied Modnar. "How do you know what I was dreaming about?"

"I was dreaming the same thing. It woke me up a few hours ago." Dambar then woke up.

"Would you guys keep it down please. I'm trying to sleep."

"We have to get started," said Bob. "Something was out there all day and I'm not quite sure what it was."

"You mean like a fox or a bear?" replied Modnar, who was now sitting upright and stretching his wings.

"You guys are *nattsu*," stated Dameron. "I didn't hear anything running around outside last day."

"That's because it wasn't running or walking for that matter," replied Bob.

"What is that smell," complained Modnar.

"It's hydrogen sulfide," stated Bob. "I noticed it last day when the bubbling noise started. It wasn't until the sun went down that I decided to take a look. It was then that I noticed that the center of the frozen lake was not frozen any longer. A vent must have become active. It melted the center and started emitting sulfide. But there was something else too. I couldn't see it but I could feel it. The only thing I could see was the smoke coming up from the vent. I need you guys to go out and find a way inside the mountain. Even if it's a small cave there might be some old lava shoots or inactive steam vents." Bob stood up and flew outside of the den. Modnar and Dameron both stood up and followed Bob.

"What are you going to do?" asked Modnar. "Dambar will need a lift to our location if he is bringing some more black powder." Bob turned his head and noticed a caribou off in the distance. He quickly took to the air and headed toward the beast. He pulled the stone from its pouch and used the line like a lasso. He spun it around in the air as he quickly approached the beast. It had its head up sniffing the air. Bob was coming up high and behind it. He went into a silent glide. As he glided over the caribou he threw down the line just in time to have the beast lower its head. The line in a big loop that was supposed to go around the head and neck instead wound up in the antlers. It got caught up in the two top tips, looped around the tips in the middle, and looped over itself with the stone hanging in the middle like a Christmas ornament on a tree. The caribou did not even take notice as he found a little plant life in the snow and began grazing on it. Bob spun around in amazement to look at the beast and then spun back around to head to the den. Once inside he sat in the center with his legs crossed and closed his eyes. The window in his mind opened and he began to see through the eyes of the caribou.

DAMBAR

Dambar made his way through the tunnels heading back home deep within the mountain. He knew he had a job to finish though. The thought of dealing with those baby spiders and its mother made him shiver. He knew they would be looking for him.

He soon found himself in the section of the caves that had the cul-de-sac with the spider's den in it. There were many cul-de-sacs in the area and he began to investigate them to double check the area before he addressed the spider issue. He was deep in thought as he went from cul-de-sac to cul-de-sac taking note of the rough black walls and the openings leading away from the main cave. Each one was different. Some had almost square-shaped fronts with ledges and some had rocks randomly placed around and inside.

One of the entrances to a cul-de-sac in the area had a pile of rocks that had apparently fallen from the overhead of the cave and blocked the entrance. Two large boulders had fallen to the left and the right of the caves original entrance. A fairly large rectangle shaped boulder had fallen horizontally across the top of the two larger boulders. It would have made a great doorway but a large amount of smaller boulders had fallen on top of that. Some fell in front of the cave entrance and a larger amount on the top of the rectangular boulder almost broke it in half. It was cracked in the center and was slowly sinking downward almost making a sort of V-shape. Dambar began to move the smaller boulders and rubble away from the entrance to make a clear path through. He noticed the scent of fresh air coming from within. He knew that the wind was very strong outside of the mountain and just a scent of fresh air meant only very tiny cracks in the cave wall was allowing the air to come through. The rocks in the front of the entrance must have been acting kind of like a brace for the upper boulder that had all the smaller rocks on top of it. As Dambar began to remove the rocks below, the V-shape of the boulder increased in angle and became more apparent. He could hear smaller rocks falling from above and the cracking sound of the boulder. By the time he had cleared the entrance the V-shaped boulder that was many feet above his head was now only a few feet above him and was getting ready to give. He wanted to search inside the cave but he did not have time. He quickly stepped in and did a quick assessment of the area and decided there were no other adjoining caves.

Dambar started to make his way to the spider's den. As he walked the sounds of shuffling and clicking filled the cave. The sound bounced off the walls and echoed off in all directions. It almost sounded like all the personalities of schizophrenic were whispering a warning to him all at the same time in a low breath of a foreign tongue. He knew the tunnels very well though and proceeded with great confidence. He had a game plan and was going to stick to it. He also wanted to get this over with and get on to better things. The direction from which the confusing echo's originated became more apparent as he came closer to the cul-de-sac. As he reached the entrance of the den he could hear a hissing sound. He flashed back to when the spiders were upon him and the sound that was produced by their acid burning away at his clothing. The sound of shuffling was soon replaced totally by the hissing sound and the smell of acid burnt flesh. They were feeding on something, what he did not know. There should not have been anyone in the caves until he had cleared the way making things safe. He pressed himself up against the cave wall and did a kind of sideways stealth walk into the den. Smoke of the burning flesh became more apparent and he could actually see it going past him. He covered his mouth and nose with his sleeve, however, the perfume on his clothes was still present and that smell mixed with the burning flesh overwhelmed him. As he breathed in his throat collapsed and his nose burned. He let out a cough and a sneeze at the same time. The hissing sound stopped and the cave became quiet again. He froze hard against the cave wall and listened. He could hear a faint clicking sound. It sounded like one of the spiderlings was coming down the tunnel. It was getting closer and closer. He could barely make it out and was hoping that it would stop and turn around. Soon the spider was right in front of him and it did not see him. He began to observe the spider. He thought how hideous they looked. He could see the tube that encircled the top of its pulsating abdomen with venom. Its venom was low and he could see it moving around inside the tube. Its tiny fangs still dripped with blood. He could see all of its eyes working independently from one another as if each one belonged to separate beings. Its scan was systematic though and started at one end of the cave. It worked its way from one side to the other and up and down. Dambar could see soon all of its eyes would be in his direction. He bent his knees down as far as he could go, kept his center of gravity, and jumped into the air. The poor spiderling did not even see him coming as he landed directly on the spiderling with both feet. It let out a tremendous scream as all the air was forced out of it. Spider goo, blood, and acid sprayed everywhere. The acid was all over his shoes and they began to smoke. A giant scream came from down the tunnel as the mother spider realized what had happened. Suddenly there were hundreds of tiny clicking sounds with a few larger clacking noises mixed in. He knew what was happening and he spun around on the slippery goo that was under his feet. He drew his sword and prepared himself. The window opened up in his mind and he gave control to Tobine. The first spider came into view. He raised his sword and came down hard slicing the spider in half. The goo oozed out of it like a cracked egg. There were then two of them right behind it. He did not have time to raise his sword again so he brought it sideways out to the right and swept hard to the left killing both of them in one blow. He quickly sheathed his sword. He could have sworn that he saw the eyes of the mother glowing hot with anger. He could hear the sound of clicking and clacking very loud now. He knew it was time to leave so he spun around and ran down the cave as fast as his smoking boots would take him. He flew out into the main cave and stopped. With all the excitement he could not remember from which direction he came. He spun one way and then the other. He couldn't wait any longer and just ran, for they would have him soon enough. He had chosen wisely and began to remember where he was going. He stopped and waited for them to catch up a bit before he started running again. He quickly came to the entrance of the tunnel he would lead them down. He ran partly down it and then stopped. He knelt down and picked up two hard rocks. He waited till they came to the entrance and began banging them together to get their attention. There were sparks flying from the stones as they collided with each other. The spiders stopped in front of the opening in a large group. It was the mother with all its children below her. The acid flowed heavy from the spiderlings with all the excitement. It cloaked the mother in an eerie purple mist. Dambar threw the rocks down the cul-de-sac and ran toward them. The spiders began their forward assault. Just as Dambar reached the front of the spiders he jumped to the right halfway up the cave wall. Planting his right foot on a small ledge he propelled himself onto a ledge in the center of the cave exit way above the spiders. The spiders continued down the cul-de-sac after the rocks. He jumped down and landed on a few more rocks that had just fallen from above the entrance. He lost his balance and came down hard. He knocked the air out of himself and was gasping for breath. The mother spider stopped and spun around. It let out a loud hiss and began to charge. Dambar rolled onto his stomach, did a pushup, gasping, and brought his feet under him. He bolted out of the tunnel and spun around. He drew out his sword and held it high over his head with both hands. He looked down to see that the spider had stopped. He knew what was coming so he came down as hard as he could on the large boulder supporting all the other stones, cracking it in half. The spider had let loose with a large web and Dambar looked just in time to see it coming in his direction. He spun around as all the boulders covered the cave entrance sealing the spiders inside. He sat down in relief as the dust from all the rocks falling blew past him in a cloudy puff.

Dambar searched his clothing for a short while before producing a small flask of green liquid. He emptied the entire contents into his mouth. With bulging cheeks, his eyes rolled back and he shook his head vigorously before gulping it down. His mind wandered back to the days of glorious battles and victories. An old tune once sung by victorious warriors in pubs during hours of celebration found his lips. He placed the flask back into a pocket and began humming the tune as he headed homeward down the tunnel. Every once and a while he would stop humming and sniff his clothing to assure himself that it was free of the earlier smell. Everything was right and he had completed his mission once again. The complications of the day's events were pushed back deep in his mind as he celebrated his small victory. He would deal with them when the time came but for now it was time to rejoice.

Soon Dambar approached the cave opening leading back into the mountain. The opening was guarded by two giant statues of mountain men on either side. Each of them held out a pickaxe, which they crossed directly over the opening. The opening itself was carved out of solid rock. It was square in shape with a two-foot-thick frame chiseled smooth and recessed five feet into the rock. All around the frame were holes chiseled out. Skulls of the people who had died pioneering the cave were placed within as observers of all who enter. In the back of the holes behind the skulls there were small holes that led all the way into the main hall. Light would travel through that hole and light up the back of the skulls giving them a life of their own. The atrium between the opening and the mountain city was hollowed out. It contained two raised fire pits of bronze, giving light, warmth, and welcoming to all those who were returning from the cold damp cave.

After passing through the atrium, Dambar began his walk through the main entrance corridor. It was built in such a manner that it would only allow a few people at a time through. This would reduce the threat of large forces making their way into the mountain city. Pressure generated in the city forced wind through the tunnel, which brought with it the welcoming smell of the city. At the end of the corridor was a very large chamber with a few weapons of defense against would-be invaders. Each wall of the chamber contained entrances to different parts of the city. Directly in front of the corridor across the chamber was the entrance into the second district. The right wall and the left wall had entrances into the first district. The first district was the lesser of the society, which encircled the second district, which was the middle class, and it encircled the third district, which held troops, the leaders, and advisors.

Dambar preferred the first district. He hated the pomp and circumstance of the inner city and the second district with all the children running around. In the first district he could be himself and people respected him. He liked to stay in his little section of town and couldn't care less for the rest of the city.

As Dambar entered the chamber at the end of the tunnel, he made a right and passed through the opening and into the first district. It was always darkest at the beginning of a district and got brighter as you got closer to the center of the activities. The shops and taverns closest to the entrance of the city were some of the seediest. Like what you might find in shipyards or near loading docks. Travelers from other cities who knew of the mountains often would stop for the night or a few days rest before continuing onward. He had a ways to go before he would reach his dwelling on the other side of the city. The first of the businesses were coming into view. On the left-hand side were a few taverns, on the right were some inns and shops for travelers. A few torches on either side of the doorways in each of the establishments kept the hallway lit. There were no fancy reflective metals imbedded in these hallways. They say that it's easier on the eyes that way. Most people's eyes are used to the darkness of the tunnels and need to adjust slowly. All the fancy shiny metals and stones would light the halls brightly. He stopped for a moment, lifted up his right arm and sniffed his clothes to see if he still reeked of perfume. He lowered his arm and his eyes roamed the area to see if anyone was looking. Everyone seemed to be going about their own business paying him little or no attention when something caught his attention. Outside one of the taverns in the area there was a petite young woman whose skin had not seen the sun in some time. She was singing a hypnotic tune. She wore a dark copper-colored dress with a tight black corset and a black shawl around her shoulders. Her black hair was long in the back with bangs that almost covered her large green eyes. Upon her head she had a small lace bonnet that laid flat and almost looked as if it was made out of spider webbing. Upon her right shoulder was a hummingbird whose feathers seemed to be reflecting a rainbow in shimmering water. The doorway into the tavern was dark and above it sat a figure with wings. As he walked toward it he realized it was one of those statues that he saw in the tunnels that resembled the creature he had fought. It was then that he began to take notice of the song the woman was singing. "Dambar, we know what you have seen," the voice came out so sweet and slow like an angel was singing. He looked in her direction as she went on. "Your fragrance is so sweet," Dambar growled in a low tone. "Inside we wait for you to meet. So many plans to contemplate so see me inside before it's too late." She never looked at him once and seemed to be staring off into space. The hummingbird flipped its wings once or twice but never left her shoulder. Dambar looked around to see if anyone was watching. Nobody but him seemed to be catching on to her lyrics. He theorized that it was because it was intended for him and him alone. He looked at the door to the entrance, which was a green oxidized copper. The door handle was shined brass and was cold in Dambar's hand as he pulled the door open.

The tavern had a low light and was very busy with games of chance, eating, and drinking. Barmaids were about distributing ale and food. In one of the corners of the tavern was a woman on a small stage singing a beautiful song of little significance. Dambar looked at her and saw that she looked exactly like the woman outside of the tavern. So much so that he had to look outside. When he looked he discovered she was gone. Upon his reentering he noticed a man by himself looking in Dambar's direction and laughing. Dambar recognized him, it was Tobine and he was dressed as a commoner to draw little attention to himself.

"You have looked better," commented Dambar as he approached and sat down across from Tobine.

Tobine laughed again and said, "I'm glad to see you finally after your excursion. Tell me please, who was that person that I saw?"

"He is a Winged," replied Dameron.

"A Winged eh. Does he have a name?"

"His name is Bob."

"How long have you known him for?"

"For a few years now," replied Dameron.

"Why have you not told us of him?"

"He did not wish it."

"Please tell me if he is a risk to us. We must keep the caves safe."

"He is no risk to us. He has helped me from time to time to keep the caves safe. The only thing he has asked in return is that I keep him unknown and allow him to stay in the caves every once and a while."

"Hmmm," replied Tobine. " I have kept this to myself thus far, your secret is safe with me. What does he do in the caves?"

"He sleeps during the daylight months."

"Are there more of them that are like him?"

"I do not know how many of them there are," replied Dameron. "I have seen two others though."

"It's strange that I have not seen anything like them before. I wonder where they came from," said Tobine. "It was a very interesting experience that we had in the cave. I have never seen anyone like that before and in such a matter as this through the stones. Who could have known it was possible. Is there any way I could meet this person?"

"There might be a way," said Dambar. "He has a very interesting proposition."

"Really," replied Tobine.

"Yes, he wishes to obtain some blasting powder to blow out Cerberus. He said that he would give us the mountain to colonize in return, but he did not say what would be in it for him."

"This is most interesting," stated Tobine. "I will talk with the others and get back to you. Here is your payment and as usual a credit line has been opened at your favorite inn that will keep you going for a while." Dambar took Tobine's sword from his side and laid it on the table. He then grabbed the bag of coin and placed it on his side where the sword used to be. He looked over to the woman that was singing in the corner. Tobine began to laugh again. Dambar looked at him and began to laugh as well. They both rose and slapped each other on the shoulder and departed.

Dambar made his way through the first district. He was not in any hurry so he followed the first district all the way around the outskirts of the city. His thoughts were replaying what he had talked to Bob about over and over again. He tried to come up with different reasons why Bob would want that mountain, just to make sense of it all.

He soon found himself in the busy hallway with all the merchants and the reflected light of green and blue. It seemed busier than usual. There were people laughing and children running about. A few of the children ran in front of him, causing him to stop quickly. He looked up as it came upon him why people were not keeping their usual distance. He just shook his head and muttered a few choice words under his breath. He soon found himself at the doorway of his favorite place. It was so out of place with all the decorations around and it was as plain as could be. He pushed the door open and walked in. The noise of the city was replaced with clinking sounds of glass and silverware. A low volume of conversations being shared was just a bit louder than the waterfall on the far side of the room. He breathed a deep sigh and walked over to the bar. He waved his thumb and index finger at the bartender and he was given two tall mugs of green brew. He lifted the mug to his mouth and gulped the whole thing down in a manner of seconds. He slammed the mug down and wiped his ale saturated beard with his sleeves. He picked up the second mug and took a long drink of it, this time actually taking the time to taste it. He began to think of what he and Bob had discussed. He picked up his ale, stood up, and began to walk to his quarters. Walking down the hallway he noticed the door to his room was cracked open. Upon reaching his door he pushed it open slowly. He peered inside and noticed it had been cleaned. His bed had fresh sheets and the floor had been swabbed. He walked in and noticed there was a small pear-shaped bottle on his dresser. It was purple and had a small crystal stopper on the top. He picked it up in disbelief as the odor of the perfume that he was doused in earlier reached his nose. He set it back on his dresser and mumbled to himself as he headed to his rack. He pulled back the heavy quilted covers and climbed into it. He pulled the sheets over his face and quickly fell asleep.

Dambar had been asleep for many hours when a petite lady, in a copper dress, wrapped in a short black cloak that covered her face, opened his door slightly and peered inside. Dambar lay on his back snoring so loud that he did not hear her entering his room. The hummingbird on her shoulder rose into the air as she walked and followed her just inches away from her shoulder. She approached his dresser and produced a fifteen-pound bag of black powder, which she placed next to the perfume bottle. This powder was a product of the mountains. It was discovered by the pioneers of the mountains. It proved to be so powerful that they used it as blasting powder to blast through solid rock and hollow out the mountains for habitation. She then began to flow silently out of the room. When she reached the door she looked back at Dambar. She grinned, lifted her hand to her shoulder, and extended a finger. Immediately the hummingbird flew over and perched on her finger. She whispered something to the bird and giggled softly.

Dambar began to dream. He stood high on a mountain top in a grand entranceway, which he had never been in before. He looked down on many mountaintops covered in snow. He then realized that all he could see though were the tops of mountains. It was as if they were small mountains floating on a sea of blackness. He looked down the face of the mountain from which he stood. The mountain he was on also disappeared into a blackness that seemed to lap at the side of the mountain like black water lapping at the shoreline of a lake. The moon shone brightly in the night's sky but its light did not penetrate the blackness below. His eyes left the mountainside and began looking out into the blackness. He noticed something had emerged from within it. It rose up high in the sky above him and then plummeted straight for him. He looked to his side but there was no sword. He tried to move his feet but could not. All he could do was watch as it came ever closer. He could hear it emitting a low sound and before he could do anything it was right in front of him producing a wind that blew upon his face.

His eyes blinked wildly as he awoke from the dream with a gasp. The hummingbird was hovering right above his face. It zipped up high and then down low again. It then zipped around in a circle as Dambar sat up. He looked at his open door as the hummingbird zipped out of the room. His eyes wandered around his room until they reached his dresser. He noticed the bag on top of it. He could smell the powder within the bag and knew what it was. He laid his head back on his pillow and began thinking on how he was going to meet with Bob. He sat up and scratched his head. He looked again at the bag on the dresser, then at the drawers and began pondering getting dressed and heading out. He stood up and began walking over to the dresser when a flash caught his eye. He stopped and looked down along the side of the dresser. He knew in a second what it was as the gleaming steel followed his eyes downward. He opened the top drawer of his dresser and froze. He could not believe his eyes. He had always taken pride in the way he placed his clothes in his drawer and he always made sure they were only warn once or twice before he would wash them. These, however, were freshly washed and folded. He took the top layer of clothes out and threw them to the floor in disbelief. He looked again and sure enough, the second layer of clothes were cleaned and folded also. He slammed the drawer shut and opened the drawers below it. He pulled out the top layer of clean folded clothes and realized that the first drawer had contained shirts and now this drawer was all pants. At this point he began to feel truly violated. He threw the pants to the floor with his shirt and began stomping on them. He rolled around on them and then threw them at the open doorway. He walked over to the door, grabbed his clothes, and looked down the hallway. Without taking his gaze off the hallway he grabbed the door and slammed it shut.

He then emerged from his dwelling with a fresh set of clothing with only a few creases and lightly covered with dirt from the floor. Slung over his back was the black powder and on his side was the sword. As he walked through the tavern he was amazed that no one was paying him the slightest attention. It was when he was halfway through the place when all of sudden it got quiet. He just kept his head down and maintained a low grumble. As soon as the patrons realized that he was okay and this was just a new look for him, the patrons carried on with their business. He flung the entrance door open and merged in with the people in the hallway. He hated having to go around people and pay attention to where he was going. This was not him and he did not like it. He didn't know what he was going to do if every time he left his place someone cleaned up everything. Who was doing this anyway? It could have been anyone. The rulers perhaps, they took great pleasure in the fact that he reeked of perfume the other day. The perfume in the room too, who would give him that, it's so expensive and besides he did not like it.

He soon found himself at the entrance to the caves. The thoughts of his previous encounters weighed on his mind. He began working his way inward leaving the light from the city behind. As he sat waiting for his eyes to adjust to the darkness the smell of hydrogen sulfide reached his nose. He knew he would have to watch his step as he moved on through the cave. There were many spots that pooled with sulfide when the area became active. He began thinking of the poem that was taught to him when he was growing up. He spoke it aloud in a low growling tone, "Deep from the depths of earth's fire does hell's wrath transpire. Within sulfide will the daemon ride to keep your soul from the grave and make it his warring slave."

COMMITTED

Just outside the cave the wind blew drifts of snow so thick that Dambar could not see far beyond the entrance. Every once in a while the drifts would thin out and he could barely make out a form or a shape of something. It was large and looked as if it was a moose with huge antlers. As he got closer he noticed that it was a very large caribou. He stopped just short of the entrance. The head of the creature seemed to be separated from its body. It was looking around as if it sensed something. It then turned its head sideways and brought its neck in and looked right at him. It then lowered its head as if to show him its antlers, which had a line wrapped around them with a stone suspended in the middle. It then raised its head and bugled so loud that it caused his eyes to vibrate within his skull. It then shook its head wildly, which caused him to realize that its head was not separated from its body, but its neck had a white fleece that was invisible in the blowing snow drifts. He began to realize that this was not an average caribou. It slowly walked toward him. As it neared him he began to walk backward deeper into the cave. When he and the caribou were both inside the cave he stopped. The caribou then kneeled down on both front knees and looked up at him. "Bob?" he questioned out loud. The caribou snorted and nodded its head in approval. He came around to the side of the caribou and stroked its back with his hand. The creature felt warm and he thought it would make a good ride so he carefully climbed on its back and held on to the white fleece of its neck. The caribou then rose up. He struggled to maintain his balance and pulled on the fleece of the caribou. It shook its head wildly and it spun around. "Okay Bob, be nice," demanded Dambar. The caribou slowly advanced toward the entrance of the cave. It stopped just short of exiting. The drifts of snow were blowing heavily and for a short second a figure of a tall man could be seen before it disappeared again. The caribou snorted and shook its head. He then came into view as he advanced. He seemed to be dressed in caribou hide. Heavy with fur, the pants were dark with lighter edges. His coat matched with a large hood that covered most of his face. As Dambar took a closer look it seemed as if the clothing was not worn, but more like fused into his skin. His face seemed to be covered by a mask that was made of a caribou skull. Upon his head were giant caribou antlers that seemed to be emerging through the hood of the coat. Dameron's face went flush. Without thinking about it his mind went back to the tales that he had heard of time and time again. Dameron's voice in an amazed tone said, "Tekkeitsertok." The figure nodded his head slowly and approached further. Now right in front the caribou he reached his hand out and closed it around the lower part of the caribou's jaw. The caribou froze and he seemed to be communicating with it. Tekkeitsertok's mind became one with the caribou. His whole body began to shake and expand as he began to take in air. He raised his head and bugled so loud and for so long as his mind not only merged with the caribou but with Bob's as well. Dameron covered his ears and closed his eyes in fear of what was about to happen. Bob as well was struck with fear and paralyzed. It was as if Tekkeitsertok was taking over Bob's mind and making him scream as his whole body shook. Bob did not count on this happening. He now realized this whole thing may have been a grievous mistake.

———————

Bob soon found himself in a place, he knew not where. He was in an opening surrounded by what looked like malnourished and crippled Christmas trees due to the ground being covered in permafrost. The trees were flocked heavy with snow and drooping over at the top. Icicles hung from the lower branches like ornaments. The air was still and the sky was alive with an aurora rainbow dancing in the sky. The silence was broken when a caribou broke through the trees. It shook its head waving its huge antlers in the air. He did not see the stone suspended between its antlers. He looked down at his side and found the pouch. He took it in his hand and felt that the stone was inside. How could this be, he thought to himself. He tried to step forward and flex his wings but he could not. It was as if he was in a dream and he could not move. A wind whispered through the trees, which shook the icicles, causing them to clang together like wind chimes, filling the air with their chaotic melody. There was no wind where he stood as large flakes of snow began falling slowly to the ground. The caribou slowly approached. He heard Tekkeitsertok's voice in his head, "You had no right taking control of that which is not yours to control. I alone have this right as I am the master of the caribou. However, I will grant you this privilege, but it will not be up to me to decide. Here before you is the caribou and it will be his choice. He must either accept you or destroy you, those are the choices that I have given the caribou."

The caribou slowly advanced toward Bob. The hooves made a low crunching sound in the snow, which got louder and louder as it got closer. The thoughts of the caribou weighed on its mind. It had seen its friends die off one by one. The caribou had seen its kind killed by wolves, by man, by bears, and even its calves taken by golden eagles. It had only been allowed to eat bird eggs, arctic char, or even lemmings, but never to just kill something. It was not in its blood to just kill without probable cause. It finally reached Bob. It raised its head and sniffed the air. Its breath puffed out of its nose like smoke from a fire. It lowered its head and took a good long sniff of Bob. Some of his hair blew in and tickled its nostrils. It let loose with a giant sneeze covering Bob in caribou goo. It then knelt before Bob. Bob reached into his pouch and produced the stone tied with line. He wrapped it in its antlers so that the stone was suspended in the center. The caribou stood up, departed into the woods, and Bob soon found himself back in his shelter.

Dambar was still frozen with his hands over his ears upon the caribou just inside the entrance to the cave. Tekkeitsertok removed his hand from the muzzle of the caribou and looked at Dambar. The wind howled outside the cave. Tekkeitsertok took a deep breath and said with a booming voice, "He has passed the test. The caribou has granted you safe passage." Dambar looked at him with huge eyes and pried his hands away from his head. Tekkeitsertok bowed his head and backed out of the cave. The wind blew a huge snow drift and Tekkeitsertok disappeared into the white void. The caribou moved forward. Dameron covered his head with the hood of his jacket and pulled his scarf across his face as they too disappeared into the snow drifts.

"*P-p-p-irrrrrrrtaaaa*," came from Dambar as they marched through the driven snow. The deafening sound of wind howled past Dambar's ears and his eyes squinted through the small gap between his scarf and hood. The snow seemed to blow past his head and swirl around in front of his face tauntingly. He marveled at the surrounding trees as they bent with the force of the wind and as the snow was blown from them they were covered up again from the trees behind them. This went on for many endless hours and miles, Dambar did not know. The wind quickly ended but the sound could be heard off in the distance.

Dambar looked up and saw the falling mountain. Gases from the magma within the mountain were escaping through the outer crust causing small avalanches all around. All the trees were now gone. They were in a pass between the falling mountain and Glacier Rivers. In front of them was a small frozen lake. Eager to reach their destination they chose not to go around. It was well into the winter season and the lake would be frozen hard with many inches of ice. As they were almost halfway across the frozen ice they began to hear what sounded like small explosions shooting out from them in all directions. They stopped and looked down to see what looked like a spider web of cracks appearing beneath them. They reached out toward the shore, like lightning bolts frozen in the sky and their thunder echoed throughout the canyon. Dambar took advantage mentally of the few seconds he realized he had left and prepared himself for an icy dip. They slowly began to sink lower and lower as the ice buckled under their weight. Dambar then noticed that there was no water coming from beneath the ice. By then though the ice shattered and they found themselves freefalling into a black void of an empty lake.

Bob screamed so loud that Modnar and Dameron, only a few hundred yards away, looked up from where they were. Just in time to have the ice break underneath them and they too found themselves falling into an empty lake. Dameron quickly grabbed Modnar from behind and wrapped his arms around his chest. "Let go," shouted Modnar, "you've pinned my wings down, I can't fly."

"I can't," screamed Dameron.

"Use your wings then," shouted Modnar. It was too late though as they fell on their backs on to the lakebed. The slope of the lakebed was very steep so as they fell they connected with it and began sliding down a slippery slope. The lakebed led them to a lava tube, which had apparently broken beneath the lake draining it of water. Modnar and Dameron's screams drowned out Bob's as they disappeared.

Dambar stopped screaming and held tight with both arms around the neck of the caribou almost choking it as they descended. By then Bob stopped screaming as well. Their echoed screams were almost visible as it left them and continued down the lava tube. It had seemed as though at one point after descending for at least a minuet they had caught up with their echoes. But these echoes were different somehow. It was not the sound of Dambar and a caribou, it was more of a high pitched screaming of a boy and a woman. Soon the steep grade of the lava tube they were in began to lessen gradually until it was almost flat. They then exited the tube and entered a large chamber as they came sliding to a stop just before a large underground pool of water. They quickly composed themselves, got to their feet, and were ready for anything that might be down there. Echoes of screams bounced all around the chamber walls. They began looking around and noticed another lava tube. They approached the tube, which made it more apparent that the screams were coming from within the tube. The screams never stopped and they came closer and closer. Both Dambar and the caribou stepped to either side of the tube.

They watched as both Modnar and Dameron came down the tube and slid to a stop just before the pool of water. Modnar looked over to Dambar with a pathetic look on his face and slapped Dameron in the face who was still screaming. Dameron's eyes opened and looked up at the caribou and Dambar staring down at them. He then released Modnar and let go a small pathetic forced laugh. He stood up and said, "That was fun." Modnar stood up as well and shook his head disappointedly looking at Dambar. The caribou's eyes were fixed on Dameron and Modnar when its lips quivered, slowly curled back, and revealed its buck-like upper and lower teeth. Its head tipped upward as if looking at the sealing while snorting in a fairly large amount of air through its snout. Its head came down, eyes widened, releasing a horrific bugle. One long bugle followed by twenty or so short, vibrated bugles. Its right leg lifted and began stomping on the ground with its hooves uncontrollably. Dambar looking at Modnar and Dameron slowly began to laugh as well, knowing that Bob somewhere was also rolling on the ground laughing.

"I don't see what is so funny," stated Dameron looking at Modnar who was looking away with his shoulders going into convulsions.

Modnar composed himself and yelled, "Cheer up," slapping Dameron in the back before losing it again. "You have to admit it was pretty fun after the fact. We are still alive after all."

"Yes, I guess you're right," agreed Dameron who was looking at the caribou who had begun foaming at the mouth before running out of air. The caribou had strings of snot hanging down from its snout, which were being sucked back up as it tried to get its breath back. This made Dameron chuckle a bit. The moment of cheer was short-lived, however, as an odor of sulfur filled the air. Everyone's eyes seemed to follow the light that filled the chamber as it began to recede back up the tunnel, as if something was chasing it. Their attention was then focused on the pool in the chamber as large bubbles the size of two-pound snow balls released small pockets of darkness. Darkness which did not seem to possess any physical characteristics, it was there but yet it wasn't. The darkness formed itself into shapes of men that crept on their backs upon the walls and floor of the chamber. They did not know what to make of this as the shapes reached out for them. Dambar soon found himself on the caribou and the Winged took to the air. Bob turned the caribou around and headed back up the tunnel from which Modnar and Dameron had fallen through. The Winged flew past them and stayed just in front of them. They could go only a hundred yards or so up the beginning of the tunnel before the incline of the tunnel became too steep. Dambar dismounted the caribou. Bob laid the caribou on its side, feet against the wall of the tunnel, and Dambar did the same just opposite the caribou. The caribou and Dambar pressed their backs together and began walking back up the tunnel that Dameron and Modnar came down. Modnar and Dameron flew up and grabbed ahold of Dambar and began pulling him up while he walked slowly in time with the caribou up the tunnel. Dameron realized that the caribou would need help as well as he noticed that its hooves did not get much in the way of traction in the cave. He flew underneath it, grabbed a hold of its hind quarters and began supporting it whenever its hooves would slip. Their eyes burned from the sulfur as they followed the nights light out of the tunnel.

Beneath the mountains that were once volcanoes were many caverns and caves connecting them all together. When the main magma source that fed the volcanoes began to cool it sealed off the tunnels with a thin layer or crust just beyond the dome from which the magma came. As rain filled the two vents just above the main dome it formed lakes that cooled the magma even further. This crust eroded and collapsed after many years of water pressure applied to it. This drained the lakes filling the tunnels below with its waters. The only water that was left was the small amount in a well as the water levels evened out within the caverns. The cooling effect the frigid water had on the magma dome began to fade as the water warmed. As the dome began to heat up it expanded and as it expanded it became less dense. This caused the water to heat up and soon became a boiling pot, shooting jets of steam through the caverns, caves, and out the once dormant volcanoes. Modnar, Dameron, the caribou, and Dambar had just made it out and had made it to the den where Bob sat just as the steam shot out of the two lakebeds simultaneously. The caribou shook its head wildly untangling the stone from its antlers and sending it to the ground. Bob emerged from the den, stopped, picked up the stone and put it around his neck. They all stood in awe as the steam shot into the sky. It seemed to go on for an endless amount of time. Bob knew that soon there would be no water pressure to keep the dome in check. This would leave the dome in a very fragile state and it would take very little for it to rupture. When it finally stopped they stood in the midst of the silence of their own thoughts. Their silence was broken by the bugle of the caribou as it took advantage of its freedom and sped off.

"What now?" asked Dambar turning his gaze toward Bob.

"We have to get this black powder down to that magma dome and ignite it," stated Bob. "This will cause the dome to erupt and send the magma through the mountain and create a volcano. And when it cools you can have the mountain for yourself. We cannot do this, however, for it is far too hot for us. We would pass out before we could even get close to it."

"You want me to go down there and do it," stated Dambar with a skeptical look on his face. Bob just stared at him with a blank look on his face. Dambar looked at Modnar and Dameron who also had the same look. Just then a loud screech filled the air as a rather large shadow darkened the spot where they were standing for a few seconds. Dameron, Modnar, and Dambar looked up in time to see Bob taking flight in pursuit of a giant Haast's eagle. It maintained what seemed to be a slow glide, which was an illusion due to its size and just seemed to be moving slow. Bob could barely keep up with it and began to wonder if he would be able catch up to it. It began to circle so Bob took note of its trajectory and cut sharply to intercept it. In his haste he did not realize where he was and flew over one of the lakebeds releasing steam. The warm updraft threw him up and off course. The warm air made him loose consciousness. When he lost is momentum with the up draft he arched forward and his limp body began a much cooler descent. The eagle still circling had no idea of Bob's presence. Bob's wings wrapped around his body as he fell facing the sky. His hair wrapped around his head and whipped his face frantically till his eyes slowly began to open. He was still woozy when his descent quickly ended on a bed of fluffy feathers. The plumage of the eagle was so thick that it didn't even notice. Bob began slipping off the backside of the eagle as the wind currents generated by the aerodynamics of the bird began pushing him off. His hands slowly began to move and he found the pouch containing the stone. His fingers wiggled the opening of the pouch until it opened enough for his hand to slip in. Grabbing the stone itself he pulled the line attached slowly out. The wind caught it and pulled it the rest of the way out. Bob rolled on his stomach and used his other hand to get a handful of feathers. The eagle screeched as Bob whipped the line around its neck just as he flew off its tail feathers. His wings caught the air and he flew up above the eagle like a kite. Hand over hand he began to real himself in until he was finally seated around the neck of the eagle. Dambar, Modnar, and Dameron's necks began to stiffen as they witnessed the event. Soon Dambar felt an uneasy feeling come over him. He looked toward Modnar and Dameron who were sporting finely tuned grins, which they had fashioned from the ones Bob had given them. So evil and malicious that he tried to force an unconvincing carefree laugh. Modnar and Dameron finally had something in common. They began laughing looking at him and then looking at themselves. They both slapped Dambar on the back and wished him good luck with a chuckle and disappeared into the den for a rest. Dambar looked toward the sky again to track Bob's whereabouts. There was no sign of Bob or the bird though.

Bob had piloted the giant bird low to the ground and behind Dambar. He swooped down inside the empty lake and as Dambar was looking skyward he came up from behind. Dambar's eyes became as a deer's eyes in a lightning storm as the giant bird popped up from out of the lakebed, floated just above his head, and dropped down in front of him. The giant bird shook, fluffing its plumage and looked directly at Dambar. Bob hopped off and glided down to the ground between the bird and Dambar, leaving the stone dangling around the neck of the bird. "Here is your ride," announced Bob in a cool yet firm tone of voice.

" I suppose there isn't any other way?" asked Dambar with his eyes as wide as gold coins.

"Nope," stated Bob. The bird's feet disappeared as it lowered its body to the ground and rested its beak on a rock. Dambar climbed the rock grabbed a hold of the line around the bird's neck and swung himself onto its neck.

"What do I do now?" asked Dambar.

"Nothing," replied Bob. "Just hold on and I will do the rest. When you get to the dome place the explosives on it and light the fuse. You will want to get back here as soon as you can. Let the bird go and hide in the shelter with us." Dambar tried to give a reply but it was cut short with his attempt to grab hold of the rope when the bird jumped into the air. It only took a couple flaps of its giant wings and it was floating above the lake and the tunnel leading down. The bird's wings closed tight around its body and it went into a dive straight into the tunnel carrying the sound of Dambar's yell with him. The sound of the wind rushing past Dambar's ears went from a light wisp to a deep hollow almost dark sound of rushing air. The bird's wings remained to its side for most of the short journey only opening a couple of times when it needed to stall for drops and turns. The dark claustrophobic feeling of the tunnel soon gave way to the open space of the chamber. The pool of water that was once there was gone and heat radiated from the empty hole. He jumped off and looked down the hole. He could only see a part of the dome itself and could see a slight glow coming from it. He knew he would not be able to go down to the dome and get out in time.

He unraveled the fuse that was wrapped around the sacks of black powder. Using it as rope he lowered the bags down to the dome. Sweat began to pour down his face from the heat and the thought of the dome actually igniting the black powder itself. He was able to rest the bags only a foot or two from the dome itself to keep it from going off. He pulled two stones from his pocket and began banging them together sending sparks toward the fuse. His hands shook with anticipation and soon the fuse was lit. The bird cawed in recognition of the completed task. Dambar wasted no time mounting the bird and exiting the cavern. He hugged the bird's neck tight and closed his eyes as it navigated the tunnel with great speed. When they finally cleared the lake Dambar did not wait for the giant bird to land. He grabbed the rope around its neck, lassoed it off, and jumped to the ground. He ran as fast as he could toward the den and made a flying leap for the opening. His thoughts reeled through his head of what would happen to them and how crazy this was. When he entered the den the first thing he saw was the smiles on the Winged faces before the ground shook with the most powerful earthquake he had ever felt. The explosion was followed by an even more tremendous explosion as the dome ruptured. The lakebeds gave way and caved into themselves, blocking the path of the gushing magma. The flow of magma flowed under the den and to all the connecting tunnels linking all the old volcanoes and truly becoming the Valley of Ten Thousand Smokes. Dambar and the Winged exited the den when they realized they were not going to die, at least not right away. There might be other actions they would need to take. They froze in their tracks once when they were out in the open. They could see the magma shooting out from the tops of all the surrounding mountains like blood spurting from the main artery of the world. Fire filled the sky with smoke and brimstone. The moon turned red before the sky darkened from the tremendous amount of smoke generated. It blotted out the moon and the sun as the whole world soon fell into an endless night. It made way for darkness, the darkness from the creature that ruled the center of the earth. Ash soon filled the skies beneath the clouds of fire and the earth turned cold in its new beginning of forever winter.

LEGEND

Within these pages contains graphic and hideous yet true facts of the art of skinning dead animals.

There are also facts on native Alaskan folklore, games, and beliefs. Most of these facts are listed within the book and can be looked up online.

Alaska Mountains in and Near the Valley of Ten Thousand Smokes:

Novarupta
Mageik
Martin
Trident,
Griggs
Alagogshak

Aurora Borealis:

You can actually hear the aurora if you are in a very quiet place. If conditions are right, you may hear some unusual noises. Witnesses have said the sound is like radio static, a small animal rustling through dry grass and leaves, or the crinkling of a cellophane wrapper. Inuit folklore says it's the sound of the spirits of the dead, either playing a game or trying to communicate with the living.

The salmonberry bush is native to the Pacific Northwest of North America and is comparable to the blueberry, only larger.

Japanese is used for the foreign words and can be looked up.

The game played by Modnar and Dameron within one of the rooms was used by the Inuit tribe in Alaska as a gambling game. It can sometimes be physically dangerous to the hands, so heavy mitts were worn while playing.

The Scientific Name of the Spider Bob Rides: Meta Menardi and Meta Bourneti:

Size:	Head and body 10 to 15 mm long
Distribution:	Found throughout the U.K.
Months seen:	All year round
Habitat:	Found in sites with no daylight such as cellars, caves, and long tunnels
Food:	Woodlice, flies, and other small insects
Special features:	There are two large brown-colored cave spiders found in the U.K.; Meta menardi and Meta bourneti. The two can only be distinguished by examining them with a strong magnifier.

They are amongst the largest spiders found in the U.K. Both species live in total darkness, so although they are not rare, they often go unnoticed.

The female cave spiders produce teardrop-shaped egg sacs, which hang suspended on a silk thread from the roof of their dwelling.

When the spiderlings first emerge they are attracted to light, unlike the adults, which are strongly repelled by light. This helps the spiderlings find new areas to colonize.

Annealing, in metallurgy and materials science, is a heat treatment wherein a material is altered, causing changes in its properties such as strength and hardness. It is a process that produces conditions by heating to above the recrystallization temperature and maintaining a suitable temperature, and then cooling. Annealing is used to induce ductility, soften material, relieve internal stresses, refine the structure by making it homogeneous, and improve cold working properties.

In the cases of copper, steel, silver, and brass, this process is performed by substantially heating the material (generally until glowing) for a while and allowing it to cool. Unlike ferrous metals—which must be cooled slowly to anneal—copper, silver [1], and brass can be cooled slowly in air or quickly by quenching in water. In this fashion the metal is softened and prepared for further work such as shaping, stamping, or forming.

Saxifrage:

The Latin word *Saxifraga* means literally "stone-breaker." It is usually explained by reference to certain saxifrages' ability to settle in the cracks of rocks.

Yukłuktaak:
Inupiaq for Snow Glasses:

Ultraviolet light reflected from snow and ice can burn the retinas of the eyes, causing severe pain and temporary blindness. Snow blindness is a threat particularly during the late northern spring, when the sun's rays grow stronger and more direct. Goggles with narrow slits reduce incoming light but still provide a wide range of vision.

Bola:

Bola is a bird hunting weapon, with seven bone and ivory weights tied to get by braided sinew. Sinew is a tough band of fibrous connective tissue that usually connects muscle to bone. The bola was designed to be thrown at a flock of birds in order to bring them down. It was used during the circa Thule period, 1200 AD to 1700 AD.

Ulu:

A half circle knife that is utilized in applications as diverse as skinning and cleaning animals, cutting a child's hair, cutting food, and, if necessary, trimming blocks of snow and ice used to build an igloo.

Ptarmigan:

A ptarmigan is the common name of birds of the Chugach Mountains in Alaska.

Tekkeitsertok:

In Inuit mythology, Tekkeitsertok is a god of hunting and the master of caribou, one of the most important hunting gods in the pantheon. Tekkeitsertok is also the protector of all the creatures that enter any parts of the northern sky. He has the power to bring aid to the creature that enters his property, or to band them from the area.

BOOK II

After the earth spewed forth its last glowing glop of molten rock and sulfur, Dambar stayed with Bob, Dameron, and Modnar. They talked over what had happened and why. Bob explained to Dambar that the Winged can only live in darkness and cold temperatures. They were tasked with the job of making it cold for a long time. With that said, Dambar went into deep thought as he looked to the black skies. He did not know what this meant for his people.

The world began to grow cold. Plummeting the globe into another ice age. The glaciers began to grow and it wasn't long before all the Winged had come to realize what had taken place.

A black sea beneath a black boat, a dark sky forever night, sails made of souls glowing a luminescent spiritual white. They were at home in the cold, a blackness that covered the world; however, they were not the only ones who flourished in the dark.

Bob admitted that he did not know that what he did would cause such devastation. He asked Dambar if he thought the mountains of which the colonies lived erupted. He looked down and shook his head. He did not know. There is one thing he did know though, and that was that the leaders would not be happy.

Most of the colonies were spared due to the way in which they had harnessed the power of the volcanoes themselves. They were not, however, capable of containing such a large blast of lava and smoke. Their safety routing system diverted most of the lava and smoke away from densely populated areas.

The lava flows were rerouted through the caves entrances, leaving the mountains, killing most of the creatures within.

The new caverns generated by the force of the lava flows allowed for the darkness from the center of the earth to come forth in greater force. It now took forms of larger enates to help recruit more souls for its cause.

A nearby fishing vessel was a three-masted schooner.

An old mirror with a reflection of the past that held prisoner a dragon in female form. If you looked in the mirror instead of seeing yourself you would see her. The background would be the reflection of where you are but in the time frame of the female who was trapped in the mirror. There is a way to get her out but it has to do with moving fast and the mirror staying still.